CROWN OF DRAGONS

A SONG FOR ORPHANS (Book #3)
A DIRGE FOR PRINCES (Book #4)
A JEWEL FOR ROYALS (BOOK #5)
A KISS FOR QUEENS (BOOK #6)
A CROWN FOR ASSASSINS (Book #7)
A CLASP FOR HEIRS (Book #8)

OF CROWNS AND GLORY
SLAVE, WARRIOR, QUEEN (Book #1)
ROGUE, PRISONER, PRINCESS (Book #2)
KNIGHT, HEIR, PRINCE (Book #3)
REBEL, PAWN, KING (Book #4)
SOLDIER, BROTHER, SORCERER (Book #5)
HERO, TRAITOR, DAUGHTER (Book #6)
RULER, RIVAL, EXILE (Book #7)
VICTOR, VANQUISHED, SON (Book #8)

KINGS AND SORCERERS
RISE OF THE DRAGONS (Book #1)
RISE OF THE VALIANT (Book #2)
THE WEIGHT OF HONOR (Book #3)
A FORGE OF VALOR (Book #4)
A REALM OF SHADOWS (Book #5)
NIGHT OF THE BOLD (Book #6)

THE SORCERER'S RING
A QUEST OF HEROES (Book #1)
A MARCH OF KINGS (Book #2)
A FATE OF DRAGONS (Book #3)
A CRY OF HONOR (Book #4)
A VOW OF GLORY (Book #5)
A CHARGE OF VALOR (Book #6)
A RITE OF SWORDS (Book #7)
A GRANT OF ARMS (Book #8)
A SKY OF SPELLS (Book #9)

A SEA OF SHIELDS (Book #10)
A REIGN OF STEEL (Book #11)
A LAND OF FIRE (Book #12)
A RULE OF QUEENS (Book #13)
AN OATH OF BROTHERS (Book #14)
A DREAM OF MORTALS (Book #15)
A JOUST OF KNIGHTS (Book #16)
THE GIFT OF BATTLE (Book #17)

THE SURVIVAL TRILOGY
ARENA ONE: SLAVERSUNNERS (Book #1)
ARENA TWO (Book #2)
ARENA THREE (Book #3)

VAMPIRE, FALLEN
BEFORE DAWN (Book #1)

THE VAMPIRE JOURNALS
TURNED (Book #1)
LOVED (Book #2)
BETRAYED (Book #3)
DESTINED (Book #4)
DESIRED (Book #5)
BETROTHED (Book #6)
VOWED (Book #7)
FOUND (Book #8)
RESURRECTED (Book #9)
CRAVED (Book #10)
FATED (Book #11)
OBSESSED (Book #12)

CROWN OF DRAGONS

(Age of the Sorcerers – Book Five)

MORGAN RICE

MORGAN RICE

Morgan Rice is the #1 bestselling and USA Today bestselling author of the epic fantasy series THE SORCERER'S RING, comprising seventeen books; of the #1 bestselling series THE VAMPIRE JOURNALS, comprising twelve books; of the #1 bestselling series THE SURVIVAL TRILOGY, a post-apocalyptic thriller comprising three books; of the epic fantasy series KINGS AND SORCERERS, comprising six books; of the epic fantasy series OF CROWNS AND GLORY, comprising eight books; of the epic fantasy series A THRONE FOR SISTERS, comprising eight books; of the new science fiction series THE INVASION CHRONICLES, comprising four books; of the fantasy series OLIVER BLUE AND THE SCHOOL FOR SEERS, comprising four books; of the fantasy series THE WAY OF STEEL, comprising four books; and of the new fantasy series AGE OF THE SORCERERS, comprising five books (and counting). Morgan's books are available in audio and print editions, and translations are available in over 25 languages.

TURNED (Book #1 in the Vampire Journals), ARENA 1 (Book #1 of the Survival Trilogy), A QUEST OF HEROES (Book #1 in the Sorcerer's Ring), RISE OF THE DRAGONS (Kings and Sorcerers—Book #1), A THRONE FOR SISTERS (Book #1), TRANSMISSION (The Invasion Chronicles—Book #1), and THE MAGIC FACTORY (Oliver Blue and the School for Seers—Book One) are each available as a free download on Amazon!

Morgan loves to hear from you, so please feel free to visit www.morganricebooks.com to join the email list, receive a free book, receive free giveaways, download the free app, get the latest exclusive news, connect on Facebook and Twitter, and stay in touch!

SELECT ACCLAIM FOR MORGAN RICE

"If you thought that there was no reason left for living after the end of THE SORCERER'S RING series, you were wrong. In RISE OF THE DRAGONS Morgan Rice has come up with what promises to be another brilliant series, immersing us in a fantasy of trolls and dragons, of valor, honor, courage, magic and faith in your destiny. Morgan has managed again to produce a strong set of characters that make us cheer for them on every page.... Recommended for the permanent library of all readers that love a well-written fantasy."

—*Books and Movie Reviews*
Roberto Mattos

"An action packed fantasy sure to please fans of Morgan Rice's previous novels, along with fans of works such as THE INHERITANCE CYCLE by Christopher Paolini.... Fans of Young Adult Fiction will devour this latest work by Rice and beg for more."

—*The Wanderer, A Literary Journal* (regarding *Rise of the Dragons*)

"A spirited fantasy that weaves elements of mystery and intrigue into its story line. *A Quest of Heroes* is all about the making of courage and about realizing a life purpose that leads to growth, maturity, and excellence....For those seeking meaty fantasy adventures, the protagonists, devices, and action provide a vigorous set of encounters that focus well on Thor's evolution from a dreamy child to a young adult facing impossible odds for survival....Only the beginning of what promises to be an epic young adult series."

—*Midwest Book Review* (D. Donovan, eBook Reviewer)

"THE SORCERER'S RING has all the ingredients for an instant success: plots, counterplots, mystery, valiant knights, and blossoming relationships replete with broken hearts, deception and betrayal. It will keep you entertained for hours, and will satisfy all ages. Recommended for the permanent library of all fantasy readers."

—*Books and Movie Reviews*, Roberto Mattos

"In this action-packed first book in the epic fantasy Sorcerer's Ring series (which is currently 14 books strong), Rice introduces readers to 14-year-old Thorgrin "Thor" McLeod, whose dream is to join the Silver Legion, the elite knights who serve the king…. Rice's writing is solid and the premise intriguing."

—*Publishers Weekly*

TABLE OF CONTENTS

CHAPTER ONE

V ars emerged onto the streets of Royalsport, gasping in the fresher air after what seemed like forever underground. He'd waited until dark to be sure no one would see him, and the waiting had been like a crushing weight on his chest, the fear pressing down on him.

He looked around on instinct, sure that someone would see him there, and know him for who he was. After all, who else had his noble features, even if they were darkened with grime from the tunnel? Yes, his frame was no more than average, his hair a dull brown that any peasant might have, and yes, he was wearing the red and purple of one of Ravin's men, but even so he felt sure that some essential kingliness, some grandeur, would shine through.

Vars set off into the city, not wanting to wait around for that to happen. Around him, the city was less quiet than he might have expected for a city under occupation. The fires of the House of Weapons' forges glowed faintly in the distance, presumably making more armaments for Ravin's forces, while the House of Sighs was lit up in a multitude of colors, as if in the middle of a festival. Presumably Ravin's men still needed entertainment, even now. Even the towers of the House of Scholars showed dots of light up their lengths. Perhaps the new emperor had them researching some new method of war.

Emperor? The thought of that made Vars want to spit on the cobbles of the street. *He* was king of the Northern Kingdom, not Ravin. Or he had been, until Ravin had made a mockery of it. Running had been the only option then.

Vars only walked now, down into the city, wary as he did so of any figure he passed. His fears told him a hundred ways he might die, his throat cut in an alley, or stabbed by some soldier's blade. He had to force himself not to skulk, to stride past the tall finery of the houses of the noble district.

He was making his way toward the edge of the city, or at least, he hoped he was. In truth, Vars wasn't sure if he could make his way across the whole city in the dark. No, of course he could. He'd been to the House of Sighs many times in the dead of night, and he'd never gotten lost. Well, not often. He'd been ruler of all of this. Of course he could find his way out.

He came to one of the streams between the city's islands. The waters were low, so Vars hurried across, not wanting to risk the bridges between. He moved into the next district, keeping his steps quiet, not wanting to attract attention. He saw the eyes of a few people out in the darkness flicker his way, and he wanted to pull further back into the shadows.

No, Vars realized, that wasn't the way to do this, not in this uniform. He strode instead, because one of Ravin's men would stride. Now it was the figures in the shadows who slunk back, keeping away from him, and Vars liked that. He was used to people looking at him with respect, and this ... this was respect.

So he strutted along the streets of the city, still heading for the walls, enjoying the way the people out in the night watched him as if he might kill them on a whim. Briefly, he remembered what it had been to be a prince, a king.

Maybe he could be again. Maybe once Vars was out of the city, he could go to the nobles, declare himself the true king, have them rise up and retake what was his. All it would take was for him to reveal who he was, and people would flock to him.

He wouldn't do it like Aethe, though. She'd been foolish, wanting to lead things from the front. It had cost her and her followers their lives. Better to set things in motion from a safe distance.

Ahead, Vars saw a work gang working by the light of flickering torches, overseen by a pair of guards. Vars couldn't see a way around, and fear briefly flared in him, but it quickly gave way to confidence. He strode past, even dared a wave because that was what he was sure a fellow guard would do. They returned Vars's greeting.

"Out alone, brother?" one of them called. "Patrols are usually pairs."

"I have a message from the emperor himself," Vars said. That seemed safer than any other lie. People gave way to kings, even quicker than to uniforms.

"Then you should hurry to deliver it," the other one began, "before ... wait, is that blood?"

He was looking down at Vars's shirt by the light of the torch, and Vars realized that while the red of the uniform might hide bloodstains at a distance, the darkness of them was showing up under the flickering light, revealing exactly where he'd stabbed the man he'd taken it from.

"I had a run-in with some rebels the other day," Vars said, trying to lie his way out of it. "Got wounded, but it's nothing."

"A wound there, and you wouldn't be walking the day after," the man said.

The other guard was staring at Vars now, looking at him with a puzzled expression.

"I know you," he said.

"Probably from the barracks," Vars said, spreading his hands. He started to back away.

"No, I *know* you."

"No, you don't," Vars insisted. He took another step back, wanting as much distance as possible.

"I've seen you, when I've been guarding in the castle. You're the joke the emperor set up in front of everyone. You're King Vars!"

He said it with a laugh, but even so, he advanced.

"What would *he* be doing out here?" Vars said. "Are you saying that I look like that ... man?"

"You don't just look like him," the guard said. He glanced over to his compatriot. "It's him, I'd swear it's him."

"King Vars, out of the castle?" the other said. It seemed to take a moment for the reality of that to sink in. "Grab him!"

Vars was already running, terror propelling him away from the two who wanted to seize him. His feet thudded on the cobbles, taking him along the street, down one turn, then another.

"Stop there!" one of the guards called behind him. Was anyone ever stupid enough to stop when a guard called that? Maybe Rodry would have turned to try to fight them, but Vars just kept running, away into the city, away to safety.

In theory, it should have been simple. This was his city, at the heart of his kingdom. Every street of Royalsport had been his once, so it should have been easy for Vars to lose his pursuers in the dark, to take twists and turns until they simply couldn't follow him any longer.

There was a problem with that, though, because it turned out that following a few well-worn routes to the noble houses of so-called friends or to the House of Sighs didn't mean that he *knew* the streets of the city. Vars was having to guess, trying to find a way to the edge by instinct.

Around him, the houses were getting poorer. Somewhere in his headlong chase, he splashed across another stream, into another district. The shouting behind him said that the guards weren't giving up their chase.

Vars didn't look back. Idiots looked back, and idiots tripped, or took wrong turns. There was nothing that could inspire Vars to run faster, because the fear was already pumping through him with every beat of his heart. He plunged on, trying to find a way out.

If this had been the noble district, maybe he might have known his way, but here, it was impossible, and soon, Vars found himself getting caught up in the tangle of streets. Worse, the guards were gaining on him. He turned another corner.

It was a dead end, blocked by carts waiting to be loaded.

Vars turned, trying to work out which way to go. Could he climb one of the carts? Could he—

A woman stepped out of a doorway. Blonde hair fell braided down her back, while her face was heart-shaped and surprisingly lovely. She was the kind of woman that Vars might have stopped to admire if he hadn't been in the middle of running for his life. Her hand grabbed at Vars, all but yanking him into the doorway she'd just come through. "Quick, in here!"

CHAPTER TWO

Meredith of the House of Sighs lay on her back in Ravin's bed, hair tousled, covered by the sheets, watching him as he stood with his back to her, wearing only the purple robes of office as he practiced with that two-handed sword of his. As he had so often in the days since Queen Aethe's death, he seemed to be completely ignoring her, now that she had provided him with his pleasures.

Meredith hated him in that moment, but she kept it off her face even though his back was turned. She knew what a dangerous man Ravin was, and how precarious her situation here could be. One glance back with her looking anything but the meek and obedient courtesan, and he would probably drive that blade through her heart.

Courtesan? Meredith held back the urge to laugh bitterly. Ravin had treated her like the lowest of whores; had made a *point* of doing so, even now that he had any woman of the kingdom he wanted at his whim. She had the bruises to prove it, all part of his game of making the mistress of the House of Sighs understand what her place in this was.

The worst part was that if he had come to her differently, she might even have liked him. Ravin was handsome enough, dark bearded and muscled, his head shaved, his eyes bright with intelligence. He was a strong, intelligent, compelling man. Meredith could see how he had taken an empire. But he was cruel with it. Meredith had felt that firsthand, but also heard it in the reports whenever she made it back to the House, of people left starving, of people killed in the street for disobeying.

Ravin came to stillness, resting the point of his sword on the floor and not even deigning to look in Meredith's direction. Still, when he spoke, the words were clearly meant for her.

"Tell me," he said. "If you could, would you kill me?"

"Of course not, my emperor," Meredith said in her most pliant tone. "I live to serve you, as do we all."

He turned, and now that those eyes were on her again, Meredith felt a brief thrill of fear.

"Of course one like you will say what she thinks she must."

"Yes, my emperor," Meredith said, dropping her gaze. "But still, I would not kill you."

Not that she hadn't thought about it. One of her girls had even offered to do it, in the privacy of her chambers back at the House, and Meredith had been forced to explain why that would be a disaster, and not just for the one to do it.

It would be easy enough. Meredith could cut his throat in his sleep or slip a poison into his drink, but what then? There was no one who could stand up to take the throne, and so there would be more war, with Ravin's armies determined to exact revenge even as different factions fought for control. For now, at least, the emperor was what stood between them and worse chaos.

She dared to look up, and saw Ravin's eyes still on her, hard and intelligent, as if guessing every thought.

"As I say," she said, "my House is there to serve you."

He smiled broadly, setting aside his sword. "I believe you. If I did not, you would already be dead."

Meredith suspected that had as much to do with all the secrets she held as with what Ravin believed about her loyalty. It was a delicate balance: he had to know that she would obey so long as it seemed like the best option for the kingdom, but that she would also work to help its people as much as she could. He'd shown that he wanted to humiliate her, and show her the place left for her in this new order, but at the same time, she was too valuable to kill.

It was difficult, and dangerous, and meant that anything Meredith did, she would have to do quietly. She had ideas forming that had nothing to do with an obvious knife in the dark, ideas that might be enough to change things, and bring down even the likes of the emperor, but it would be delicate work, and dangerous.

"Now," Ravin said. "I think it is time for you to show me again why your House has such acclaim."

As he approached the bed, Meredith forced her finest smile. "Of course, my emperor. I exist for your command."

At least, she did until she could find a way to kill him without bringing the kingdom down around their ears.

When he was eventually finished with her, Ravin stared down at Meredith's sleeping form with amusement. He had to admit that she was lovely, but of course, many women were lovely. Even now, his men would be plucking up some of the finest for him, to keep him entertained when he wasn't dallying with the mistress of the House of Sighs.

What made this interesting was that they both knew what she was, and what her House really was. This was a woman who distilled whispers until they became something sharp edged, who could send those as trained as any Quiet Man to do her work. Having one such as that at his beck and call was a big part of the excitement for Ravin.

Perhaps in time, he would do more than send for her at intervals to command her to his bed. Before that, though, he wanted to make sure that she thoroughly understood her place, that she was thoroughly his, and no one else's.

Not that there *was* anyone else, now. That had ended the day he'd had Queen Aethe executed days ago now. The would-be rebels among the nobles had been thinned out, and had no leader now, in any case. Oh, the coward Vars had fled, but who would follow a man like that? The queen's daughters were missing as well, but that simply meant that his Quiet Men had done their job with their usual skill.

So eventually, Lady Meredith would see that Ravin was the best hope this kingdom had of strength and unity. Perhaps she already did, because she was far from stupid. Then, he would have the best collectors of secrets in the Three Kingdoms at his command, there to learn everything he wanted to know about his foes and his subjects. Where until now he had ruled through overt fear, he could use the House to make things run smoothly, knowing in advance every move people might make.

That was for later, though. For now, Ravin was bored with her.

"Wake up and leave," he ordered her, shaking her awake. "Now."

She clutched her dress to her as she fled from the room, back to the place she'd come from. As she left, one of Ravin's Quiet Men entered, not even waiting for permission before he came forward and swept into a bow. The man was utterly nondescript save for a scar below his left eye. He wore simple courtier's clothes in red, and his features were bland, unmemorable. Ravin stood and swept his robes back around him.

"There had better be a good reason for this interruption," he said.

"There is, Emperor Ravin," the man said.

"I will judge that," Ravin said. "What is your name?"

"Quail, my emperor." The man bowed again. "Three bodies have been found, several days old."

"Bodies…" Ravin shrugged. "Princess Lenore and the others? If this is to report on the success of the others of your troupe, this is not the way to do it."

The Quiet Man shook his head. "Regrettably, the bodies… they appear to be those of the ones sent to kill the princess at your order."

"What?" Ravin roared. "And no one noticed? No one saw that the Quiet Men were not where they should be?"

"Eventually," Quail said, "which is when we searched, and found the bodies. But when the princesses attended the execution, it was assumed that they were biding their time, and struck after that. It was assumed that they were… taking their time."

"Of course it was," Ravin said.

"Forgive us, Emperor," Quail said, and this time he fell to his knees. "We are rarely open about our tasks, even with each other."

Ravin bit back his anger. Of course they weren't, because that was how he preferred things. The Quiet Men operated in small groups, so that they couldn't get too powerful, or start ignoring his instructions. In this case, though, it meant that the princesses had survived, and that made him want to cut the head from the fool in front of him. That would do no good though. Right now, the Quiet Man was more useful alive.

"You think that I am going to kill you, don't you?" Ravin said.

"The... possibility was raised," Quail said. There was a hesitation in his voice, but not true terror. Quiet Men had such things taken out of them in their training, in ways that even Ravin considered cruel.

"And you were the one they chose to send, even though it could have been others," Ravin guessed.

Quail merely nodded.

"Then you shall be the one to lead the chance at redemption for the failure," Ravin said.

Now the Quiet Man looked puzzled. "My emperor?"

"The princess needs to be found. She needs to die," Ravin said. He thought for a moment. "They both do, and the knight who stands by their side. They are all too dangerous to be allowed to live."

The Quiet Man hesitated for a second.

"You do not agree?" Ravin said.

"They are two insignificant girls and a madman," Quail said. "There are those... there are those who could not understand why you sent our number to murder Princess Lenore in the first place, when you could have claimed her, or had Lord Finnal control her."

Ravin snatched up his sword, bringing it around until it rested just below the Quiet Man's right eye.

"Would you like another scar to match your first?" he asked.

The Quiet Man held steady. "As it pleases you, Emperor Ravin."

"And *this* pleases me too. That should be sufficient for you." Ravin wasn't in the habit of explaining himself to his men, but now, perhaps it would help. "Princess Lenore was always a potential threat while she was here. In my Red Lodge, she would have been no danger, a mere prize to hold. Here, people might have rallied to her, and they might still. She needs to die, and quietly. None can know that she survived."

The Quiet Man nodded. "As you command."

He stood and turned to go.

"And Quail?" Ravin said, stopping him short. "Remember that I have the House of Sighs now. If my Quiet Men fail again, maybe some of you will find yourselves replaced."

CHAPTER THREE

The sun beat down on Lenore as she and the others walked. Around her, fields of wheat and barley stood moving gently in the wind, dry stone walls separating them and small drovers' tracks providing routes from one place to another. Here and there, a scarecrow stood in the fields, or a stand of trees broke up the monotony of the landscape.

They'd been walking now for days, moving carefully, keeping to the smaller paths between fields. Her legs ached with the effort, but she knew not to complain. They were lucky not to be dead right now. Compared to that, a little discomfort was nothing.

"Are you all right, Princess?" Odd asked. He'd been concerned for Lenore's well-being since they'd left the city, heading out into the countryside. He still looked strange in noble clothes, his shorn hair not suiting it, and he kept his cloak around him as if it were a substitute for his monk's robes.

"I'm fine," Lenore said. In truth, she was hungry and tired and frightened, but she would be strong. She knew how she had to look by now. Her clothes were stained and torn at the edges from catching on bramble hedges they'd had to cross. Her dark hair was tied back to keep it clear of her face, and the sunlight dazzled her eyes.

Erin walked ahead, leaning on the stick that hid her short spear. She was grubbier than either of them, because she was always the first to plunge on through streams or across low walls. There was a glint of her armor every time she moved, and her features looked set below her short hacked hair, determined not to show any of the pain that she must feel. She looked around for threats, eyes on every bush, tree, and wheat-filled field. She'd been quiet over the last few days, and Lenore didn't know whether that was about her continuing anger at them not staying to fight, or grief at their mother's death.

Lenore shared that grief, and more than a little of the anger that went with it. If she closed her eyes, Lenore could still see the moment when Ravin had raised his sword before her mother, tied helplessly to an execution stake. She couldn't escape the sight of that blade plunging into her mother, seeing the moment when she'd died over and over again. Why would it be any different for Erin?

"Can you see anything ahead, Erin?" Odd asked.

Erin didn't answer.

"Erin," Lenore said. "Is the way clear?"

"It's fine," Erin replied. She looked around, and she briefly gave Odd a hard look before she answered. "I think that there's a village ahead, past those trees. I can see chimney smoke."

Lenore looked, and there was smoke, just as her sister said. She hoped that it was chimney smoke. There were too many worse things that it could be so soon after an invasion.

"We should approach cautiously," Odd said, as if thinking the same thing.

"What's wrong?" Erin shot back. "Afraid?"

Lenore held back a sigh. It had been like this since they'd left. Before, Erin and Odd had seemed like a perfect complement to one another, in spite of the former monk's strangeness. Now ... there was tension between them. They barely trained with one another, and Erin took no part in Odd's morning meditations. Each seemed to be fine with Lenore, but the tension between them was palpable.

"We will get a good look at it as we get closer," Lenore said. "If it's burned out, we'll have to move on, but I don't think it will be. Ravin thinks he can rule, so he doesn't want to burn everything."

Just saying his name made Lenore's hands clench into fists.

"There might be guards," Odd said.

"Then we kill them," Erin shot back.

Lenore kept walking. "We'll have to risk it. We need more supplies."

Those were proving costly. Because they'd planned for this moment, they'd been able to take money with them, and jewelry that could be sold if needed, but even so, Lenore was worried that they hadn't brought enough.

"We can't run forever," Erin said.

"I could find somewhere safe for us," Odd said. "Somewhere beyond the kingdom."

Lenore stopped on the track. She had no time to resolve this, but she wanted to be clear about one thing. She stared at the others, letting them see the resolve in her.

"This isn't about running," she said. "We've escaped the city, but I will not spend my whole life running. Ravin is not going to win this, not after everything he's done. Argue about everything else if you want, but we are going to take back this kingdom."

They looked at her in surprise, but then with a hint of respect. Lenore was already walking again, though. She didn't have enough time to mediate whatever argument this was. Right then, it felt as though she'd already wasted too much time. She'd wasted it being the princess that everyone expected. She'd wasted it being meek, and obedient, and passive.

She wasn't going to do that now. It felt to Lenore as though there was a fire burning somewhere inside her, fueled by all the loss she'd felt over the last few months, all the ways she'd been betrayed, or hurt, or seen those she'd loved taken from her. Her mother was the harshest part of it, but it wasn't the only one. Her brother Rodry was dead, and her father. Her sister Nerra was gone, and Lenore didn't know if she was alive or dead. Greave was missing too, and he was not cut out to be caught in a war.

Lenore hadn't been either, but it felt as though this fire inside her was hardening something in her, like the heat from Devin's forge. Thoughts of him brought a wave of other emotions too, wishing that he was there, that he might find them. Lenore knew that she had to focus, though. She couldn't be distracted, even by thoughts of him.

They kept walking, and soon a village lay ahead, nestled between trees on one side and open fields on the other. It was small and sleepy looking, with thatched roofs and quiet gardens between the houses. There was a forge, an inn, a granary, and a small open square with a few people about their business, but little beyond that.

Lenore moved forward into the village with the others at her back. People stared at them, obviously trying to work out who they were, and if they were any kind of threat. Lenore looked around them, trying to guess if any of them might be Quiet Men. That was the hard part with what she was going to do: the moment she started to gather support, there was a risk that Ravin would hear, and strike back.

Even so, she had to do it, so she went to the middle of the village green, standing there while Erin kept her hand tight on her spear and Odd looked around for possible threats.

"Who's in charge in this village?" Lenore said, then realized that she was speaking too quietly to be heard. She could imagine her mother there, telling her to speak up, so that her voice would carry across any lord's hall. "Who runs things here?"

A man stepped forward, perhaps forty, with the weather-beaten look that came from being outside.

"I'm Harris, the miller," he said. He nodded to another man, who had to be ten years older than him, with a beard shot through with gray. "That there's Lans, the burgoman. Other than that, these are some of Lord Carrick's lands. Who are you, lady?"

Lenore took a breath, glancing from Erin to Odd for support, feeling as many nerves as she had before any courtly dance, and more. She knew how many dangers there might be in this moment, all the watchers who might be lurking, all the threats that might come from what she was about to say. Even so, she had to say it.

"I am Lenore, daughter of Queen Aethe and King Godwin the Third. I have come from Royalsport to speak with you all, to try to raise support, and to undo the damage that King Ravin has done."

The older man, Lans, looked at Lenore for a moment or two before shaking his head.

"What kind of joke is this?" he demanded. "Are you here to steal from us, or to test our loyalty? Why are you lying to us, girl?"

"No," Lenore said. "It's not a lie. I am Princess Lenore."

"Princess Lenore is dead," Lans said. "Everyone knows that. Criers came to announce it, along with the death of the queen."

He moved away, shaking his head. The miller made as if to leave with him, but Lenore stepped forward, grabbing his arm. He started to brush away, shoving her back, and Lenore saw Erin start toward him. Erin grabbed the large man, twisting his arm behind his back in a way that looked painful. That wasn't what this moment needed. She held up a hand to forestall her sister.

"Erin, let him go," she said. She could see some of the villagers around them growing restless, and could see Odd's hand going to his sword, looking out for trouble.

"But he's not going to *listen*," Erin replied.

"He'll listen," Lenore said. "But not if the only reason he's doing it is because we're hurting him. Let him go."

She did it, and Lenore breathed a faint sigh of relief. She saw the miller rubbing his wrist where Erin had grabbed him, and knew that she had only a brief moment to change his mind about them.

"If you've heard that I'm dead," Lenore said, "maybe you should think about *why* they're saying that. Maybe it's because they know that we're a threat to them. Maybe it's because we're the one chance of actually fighting back against everything that's happening. I know it's hard to believe, but I *am* Princess Lenore, and *that* is my sister, Princess Erin. You've heard that she trained with the Knights of the Spur? Do you think someone so small who *hadn't* trained with them could do that to you so easily?"

The miller looked at Erin. "Aye, maybe."

"And that is Odd," Lenore said, gesturing to where the former knight still stood ready with his hand on his sword's grip. "He used to be Sir Oderick the Mad." She saw the way the miller stared at Odd then, in obvious fear. "Would anyone lie about that? Would anyone dare to claim it, knowing how much trouble it would bring? Just by telling you who I am, I have put myself and my sister in danger."

"I ... I suppose so," Harris the miller said.

Lenore knew that she had to push now, or she would never convince him. "We are not here to lie to you, or to steal from you, but to build an army. Just gather people together, and have them listen to me. After that, it will be your choice what you do, and if you believe me. Please."

"All right," he said. "Tonight, at the inn, but I can't promise they'll listen."

"They'll listen," Lenore said. "I'll *make* them listen."

CHAPTER FOUR

Nerra stood on the terrace of the Isle of Hope's temple, watching as, one by one, the people of the island walked toward the fountain. Nerra stood by it, trying to reassure them as they walked to their destinies. Above, on the slopes, the dragons sat, their collective presence concentrating on the pool, wiping away the last magic of the curse. Shadr was at their heart, larger than any of them, a black so deep that it was like looking out into the night sky.

The other Perfected took ladles and cups, goblets and whatever other containers they'd been able to find, passing the water to the ones with the dragon sickness. For her part, Nerra took a cup, dipping it in the fountain and passing it to a young woman who looked as though she might only just have arrived on the island a short time ago, because the scale marks weren't prominent on her skin yet. By the standards of a human thing, she was slightly built and pretty, biting her lip as she considered the cup Nerra gave her.

"I'm afraid," the girl said.

"Don't be," Nerra reassured her. "This will help you. It will let you be what you were always meant to be. I was frightened when I came here."

"Will I be like you?" she asked.

Like her. It took Nerra a moment to remember what she was, looking down at the blue scales that covered her arms, feeling the claws extend as she willed it, tasting the air with senses that she could never have had before.

"You will become something amazing. Drink, all of you, drink."

They drank, all at once, some taking sips, others great gulps. For a moment, nothing happened, but Nerra knew better than to think it was just water now.

She heard the first of them cry out, saw the first of them collapse, and for a second, she *did* know fear. What if something had gone wrong? What if the curse had not truly been lifted?

Trust in us, Nerra, Shadr said to her. *Trust in me. They are changing, not dying.*

Even as the screams rose around her, Nerra could see the process happening. Bodies started to stretch and reshape, cries becoming more guttural, more bestial, as those there started to transform. How many would become Perfected and how many would be left as the Lesser?

Whichever it is, they will still be more than human things.

Nerra swallowed, knowing that it was true, yet still hating to watch as bones stretched and broke, skin tore and flowed and reformed.

Come, Nerra. Shadr's voice was soothing in her mind. *Fly with me.*

The dragon queen lowered her neck, allowing Nerra to climb aboard, her clawed hands finding purchase on the roughened scales at the dragon's shoulders. Shadr spread wings wide enough that they could have been the sails of some great ship, and rose into the air with one wing beat after another. In seconds, the Isle of Hope was far below. The ruins of the village were still smoldering.

It is hard for you to watch their pain, Shadr suggested once they were up above the island. *But that pain is a necessary part of things changing. They will be more, much more, when it is done.*

"I know," Nerra said. The wind whipped at her words, but she knew that the dragon would hear them. "It still hurts to watch them."

You are kind, Shadr said to her. *But you must also be strong. In the battles to come, you will need to be.*

"I will be," Nerra assured her. "When will we fly there?"

Soon. Soon the world will be as it was again. As it must be.

Nerra had seen what that world would be, and what it had been. It had been beautiful, with the dragons ruling, and the Perfected serving as conduits between them and the mass of humans. Yes, there was still a part of her that seemed to have some tiny nagging doubt, but Nerra ignored it, because it made no sense. Of course this was what should happen.

There is something that must happen first, though.

Shadr wheeled down toward the ground, landing on an empty patch of beach. Nerra slid down from her back and then stared up at her.

"What? What has to happen?"

There is a threat that sits large in our kind's memories of the human things' rebellion, an object that evened the odds for them, turned brood-kin against one another. They could not fight us with their own strength, and so they produced a trick, a thing to corrupt us.

Nerra could barely believe that anything could stop the dragons, yet if it was true, and something like that was out there, it was a huge danger.

"Show me," she said.

Shadr inclined her great head slightly, and images washed over Nerra.

She watched as human things marched out against the masses of dragons. She saw some of them burn, some of them fall torn apart by claws, or tail swipes. She saw lightning and fire and more pour down over them. She saw the ranks of the Lesser flood a field so vast that it seemed to stretch all the way to the horizon. For a moment, it seemed that the rebellion would be put down, and the natural order of things resumed.

Then a man stepped forward, something clutched in both his hands as if it were too precious to even risk dropping. It shone with jewels in the varied colors of the dragon kin, and a scale sat at the center, reflected in the light of dragon flame. Nerra knew without being told that it had come from one of the most powerful of their kind, gathered from a former dragon queen by hands that had smuggled it away when the scale had fallen in a fight.

Nerra saw the moment when the first of the Lesser threw themselves back from that amulet. She saw worse, though, because dragons them-selves banked in their flight, and now the deadliness of their breaths fell on the Lesser, and even the Perfected.

Then they started to turn on their own kind.

Images flashed together in Nerra's mind now, with moment after moment of dragons flying at one another, not just in the battle, but again and again beyond it. She saw them strike at one another from the blue sky, plunging like hawks on waiting doves and tearing at leathery wings with claws too sharp to resist. Sometimes the attacking dragons fell, but the human things wouldn't care about that; it was just one more dead dragon to them.

The horror of it continued. Nerra saw dragons fighting in terrifying tangles in the sky, saw the air filled with fire and poison and ice. She saw younglings slain by older dragons, saw dragons lead human hunters toward the wounded to finish them. Nerra cried out at it, not wanting to watch more, not able to stand the blood and the death of creatures so beautiful, so powerful. How could the human things do something so evil as to kill them, when they were weak, cruel things in comparison to dragon-kind?

Nerra came back to herself with a gasp of anguish. She was lying on the beach, Shadr standing over her, pity flowing from the dragon to her.

"How...how could they do it?" she demanded. "They have to be stopped!"

They will be. Things will be restored, but for that, the amulet must be destroyed.

And for that, they had to find it.

"It isn't out in the open," Nerra said. "It's not something anyone has told me about."

I know, Shadr said. Of course she knew, when the two of them were so connected. *But you know the kingdoms of the human things. Where would they put an object of such power?*

Nerra tried to think, but the sheer number of possibilities was over-whelming. A thing like that could be hidden anywhere after so long. A nobleman might have it as a trinket, or it might have been stolen and stolen again a hundred times over the generations. Human lives passed so quickly that it might have been placed in a box and forgotten, buried and lost.

If it is lost, then it is not threat, Shadr pointed out. *But it will not be lost.*

"A lot of the knowledge of dragons has been," Nerra said. "People know they exist, or existed, but they treat them like they were always a long way off. They treat them almost like myths."

There are those who know, Shadr insisted. *The watcher on this island was set here for a reason, and there are those who would have made sure that the knowledge was not lost. This is too powerful a magic to forget.*

"There might be collectors of magical things," Nerra said. "There are always those who dabble in magic, even beyond the royal sorcerer. Any one of them might have it."

Perhaps.

That didn't feel right though, and even without Shadr's prompting, Nerra knew that it wouldn't have worked like that. She tried to put herself in the mindset of the humans from so long ago. What would they have thought? What would they have done?

"The ones who won the war would have been the new rulers," Nerra said.

I cannot remember what none of us were there to see, Shadr replied.

"No, they would have been. Or the people who *did* rule would have known the importance of a weapon like that. They would have held onto it, but with a magical thing like that, they would have given it to those who might use it."

Suddenly, the possibilities seemed far narrower. Who would maintain the knowledge of the dragons? Who would maintain knowledge of magical things, but still be ready when the king called on them? Nerra could only think of two possibilities.

"Either the king's sorcerer has it or the House of Scholars does," she said. "If it's the magus, he'll have it in his tower in Royalsport. If it's the Scholars ... they have a House in Royalsport too, but something like this ... I think they would hide it in their library in Astare. Greave used to talk about it. He wanted to go there some day." It was strange, thinking of her brother like that, now that she was so far beyond anything human.

We must choose where to search, Shadr said. *I do not like the idea of going to the magus's city first, or to the place of kings. There is too much risk in that.*

"Then we go to Astare?" Nerra asked.

The dragon blew a whisper of shadow up into the sky. *We go to Astare, and we take the one thing that could stop us.*

CHAPTER FIVE

Greave stared out eagerly as the coast of the Northern Kingdom came into view. He suspected that he was a different man than when he'd left, and not just because his delicate features were roughened now by a darkening beard, because his dark hair was tangled by the wind, or his slender frame had hardened a little through the effort of travel.

He suspected that even his own family wouldn't recognize him, although the sailor behind him had, eventually. He had never thought that he would feel so much joy at the sight of home, or such worry. If the sailor who was piloting him home was to be believed, so much had changed since he had left.

He'd seen the start of the invasion for himself, in Astare. If Royalsport was like that ... then he had to do something about it. He'd set off trying to save his sister, and he still had the means to do it tucked into a vial in his belt. Now though, there were more people who needed saving, and Greave wasn't sure if he had the skills to do it.

"How long before we reach land?" Greave asked the man, who stood with a determined hand on the tiller.

"Not long now. Are you *sure* you don't want to just head back to the island?"

Greave wasn't going to pretend that he wasn't tempted. On the island where he'd washed up on his makeshift raft, there had been more than enough food, water, and shelter to survive indefinitely. It would have been the easy thing, the safe thing, to just stay there and wait out the war, only slipping back when it was all over.

That would mean abandoning everyone he loved though. His sisters. Aurelle ...

Her name crept into his thoughts without him meaning to. In spite of all she'd done to betray him, in spite of the fact that she'd been sent to kill him, he couldn't help the swell of love that came when he thought of her. No, he would focus on the others, on his family.

Greave stared out as the coast came closer. The sailor brought them into a secluded inlet, with what looked like a rough-hewn path leading up. Greave felt the scrape of the boat on the stones below and hopped down, grateful to feel the ground under his feet again. He turned, setting his hands to the boat, ready to help push it off.

"Thank you for this," he said to the sailor. "Thank you for bringing me home."

"Don't thank me," the other man said. "I've probably brought you back to your death."

"Nevertheless," Greave said. "If we both get through this, seek me out, and I will see that you're rewarded for your help. I keep my promises, and I help those who help me."

"You're not too far from Royalsport now," the sailor said. "Head inland, and you'll find a road soon enough. Then head south and you'll be there in a day or two."

Greave nodded. He helped to shove the boat back off the shale shoreline, and the sailor started to row it back out enough that he could use the sail again. Greave watched him go and then turned, wanting to make as much progress toward Royalsport as he could before dark.

He clambered up the small path from the shore, finding himself on grassy upland as he came to the top of a small cliff. There were trees and fields in the distance, and something that might have been a small trackway a little way off, leading toward both. Greave started to follow it, reasoning that it was probably his best way of finding a larger road, and then a route to Royalsport, and his family.

He wasn't sure what he would do when he got there, so Greave started to apply his mind to the problem. His mind had always been his greatest asset; he'd managed to recreate a cure for the dragon-sickness on an island with no resources. If he'd managed that, couldn't he manage to work his way through this problem, as well?

It wasn't a problem though, it was a war, an invasion.

No, Greave told himself, that didn't matter. Or rather, it was too big, too overwhelming, to *allow* it to matter. Think about the sheer overwhelming impact of a war, about the death, about the terror, and he wouldn't be able to think well enough to decide on what to do next.

Greave knew about problems. The philosopher Araxon said that the appropriate way to deal with a problem was to break it into a series of smaller problems, dividing and dividing until there were steps small enough for a human being to take. Of course, his rival Xero had written that the true complexity of problems could only be understood in their entirety, but Greave didn't think that was helpful right now.

As for war, there had been as much written on that as on almost any other topic in human history. Greave had read the works of the major tacticians, understood the principles of what he was going to need to do. He'd read works on politics and statecraft, histories of the rulers who had come before. He hoped that some part of it would provide him with the answers he would need.

For now, he kept walking, trying to find the right way. He kept thinking as he went, kept picking at the great problem that threatened to kill them all. What was the first thing? Greave knew the answer to that instinctively: he didn't have enough information. He didn't understand the full scope of what was happening, didn't know enough of the details to begin to decide what to do.

He needed to find out where his family were, and what had happened to them. He couldn't do anything to save them if he didn't even know where they were. That was the first thing, but others spread out after them in a seemingly impossible cascade. He would need to know what all the different groups were in the kingdom, who ruled where, what loyal forces remained . . .

Greave was still thinking about all of that as the small track he was on gave way to a larger road, leading through a wooded section. Travelers started to pass him on the road now, some moving with sacks of belongings, others carrying weapons. They all gave Greave wary looks, staying away from him. At first, he flinched, thinking that they'd worked out who he was, but then he realized that it had more to do with how wild he looked, disheveled and probably dangerous.

"Am I on the right road for Royalsport?" he called out to one of them, a man struggling under the weight of whatever belongings he'd been able to snatch up. He was a little taller and broader than Greave, dressed in clothes that were simple but well made.

"Just that way," the man said, nodding the way Greave was going. Greave was grateful for that, because at least it meant that he wasn't wasting his journey.

"Thank you," Greave said. "You've been very helpful."

Even as he said it, he saw the other man staring at him.

"I know that voice," he said.

Greave started to back away slightly, caution rising naturally in him. He didn't want to be recognized, not here, not now. He stared at the other man, trying to work out how he could possibly know him.

"I thought you were familiar when I saw you, but the voice. I used to work at the castle, and I heard you once, reciting poetry in the gardens."

Those words hit home far too closely.

"You're mistaken," Greave said. "You don't know me."

The other man took a step forward. "I do. You're Prince Greave."

Fear flashed through Greave at the moment of recognition, but he held that fear back. He couldn't let this man see any reaction.

"You're mistaken," he said. "What would Prince Greave be doing out on a road like this?"

"I'm not wrong," the man said. He was staring hard at Greave now. "Your clothes are too rich for any peasant's and your face is the same, in spite of that beard."

The fear started to harden into something else inside Greave. He couldn't be found, not now, not yet. He needed time to work out what he was going to do, and to get to his family. If this man told anyone what he'd seen, if he mentioned it to the wrong person, then Greave was going to be in a lot of danger.

"It's vital that you don't tell anyone about this," Greave said, knowing that there was no point in trying to deny it anymore. The other man had made up his mind, and nothing was likely to convince him otherwise. What did that leave? An appeal to his loyalty? "If you care at all about this kingdom..."

"What kingdom?" the other man shot back. "It's all fallen to Ravin. Even the rest of the royals have been killed by him."

Those words made pain flood through Greave, sharp and sudden, seeming to numb everything else. He didn't know how to react in that moment, didn't know what to say or do.

"No, that can't be true," he said. He couldn't accept it, wouldn't accept it.

"I saw Queen Aethe's execution with my own eyes, and they announced the deaths of Princess Lenore and Princess Erin a day after. Doesn't take a genius to work out what happened there. Quiet Men."

"No, you're wrong, you're lying," Greave said, because the pain of his grief was too great for that. It mingled with an anger that surprised him, that must have been building inside him this whole time.

He started toward the other man, and now there was a knife in his hand.

"I'm not lying. There's just you left, Prince Greave. At least, until someone tells the Quiet Men where you are."

He knew how dangerous this situation was for him, and he could almost hear Aurelle's voice, telling him what the obvious solution was, telling him the only way out of all of this.

He had to kill this man, before he told anyone.

Greave saw the man start to back away, but he was still close enough that Greave could have lunged forward and buried a blade in him easily. Aurelle would have done it, but Greave... he couldn't do it. There were still better ways to deal with this. He could offer the man money, reason with him, think his way out of this. He wasn't a murderer.

In the second that Greave hesitated, the other man ran, setting off into the trees. Greave stared after him in shocked disappointment, and then, not knowing what else to do, he set off after him.

CHAPTER SIX

L enore waited in the inn while Odd looked it over cautiously, apparently trying to think of all the ways that someone might be able to hurt her there. Lenore wasn't sure how much there was to see. It was a large, open room with a few tables and benches, a few casks at one end and little else.

Erin, meanwhile, sat with her, nursing a small beer and picking at a hunk of bread and cheese. Occasionally, she looked over at Odd, and the look wasn't friendly.

"What is it between you two?" Lenore asked.

Erin looked away, not answering.

"Erin..."

"I'm not your subject to order around, Lenore," she snapped.

Lenore put her hand over her sister's. "No, you're my sister, and I care about you. I worry about you."

"You don't need to worry about me," Erin said. "Just about the people who get in my way."

Lenore sighed. She didn't know what to say to the anger that sat inside her sister, and that came out so often now. She had a trace of the same anger, but it wasn't the blazing thing that threatened to consume everything around Erin.

She couldn't think of anything that she could say or do that might help. Maybe if they succeeded in winning back the kingdom, that would be enough, but Lenore knew how long a road it might be to that point, and she knew that she couldn't hold Erin's hand the whole way. She just had to hope that being there for her would be enough.

For now, people were starting to come into the inn, men and women straggling into it in ones and twos. There weren't that many, because it wasn't a large village, but it was still enough that slowly the inn started to fill, tightly packed as the castle's great hall might have been for an audience. People glanced over at Lenore and her sister, obviously having heard who they were, coming to see what would happen, even if they didn't quite believe it.

In a village like this, getting people there was the easy part. Lenore was something to see, perhaps something to talk about later. The hard part was how she was going to be able to use this moment. This was like setting a taper to kindling, and now it would either catch or fizzle into nothing.

That made the things Lenore was about to say more important than anything she'd said in her life. In truth, she was starting to realize that most of the things she'd said or done before hadn't mattered very much.

That was a hard realization. For so much of her life, she'd thought that she was the responsible one, the one doing the right thing by being the princess everyone expected her to be, but how much good had that truly done in the world? She'd been a pretty ornament at the court, there to be married as soon as possible to reinforce the bonds between the crown and one of its most important lords. She'd been there to be courteous, and welcoming, but nothing she'd said had ever truly mattered to most of the people around her. Not to her husband, not to the courtiers, not even, truly, to her mother.

Now, the things she would say would make or break her cause.

Erin offered her a sip of her drink, but Lenore was too nervous for that. Besides, she needed to keep a perfectly clear head. She needed to sound certain and confident, every inch the ruler people would need to see her as if this was going to work.

"You can do this," Erin whispered to her, when the inn was nearly full.

Lenore nodded, trying to make herself believe it. She stood, then clambered up onto the table so that everyone could see her. It was time.

"Thank you for coming," she said, raising her voice. "My name is Lenore. I am the daughter of King Godwin the Third."

She paused for a moment to let that sink in, occasional gasps coming from around the room. Only a few, though, because it seemed that enough people had heard her on the village green for the news to start to spread.

"My father is dead," she said, holding back the grief she felt. "My mother is dead, and my eldest brother."

"We heard *you* were dead!" someone called out from the back of the crowd.

"That's the rumor King Ravin has put out," Lenore said. "And why? Because I and my sister Erin are the last people opposition to him might gather around. My sister Nerra and my brother Greave are missing. My other brother, Vars, is a coward who murdered his own father, and who serves as Ravin's puppet."

That got more of a reaction, with murmuring spreading through the crowd. The man who'd called out before wasn't done, though.

"How do we know you're who you say?" he demanded.

"Do you think anyone would truly impersonate *me*?" Lenore shot back, with a bitter laugh. "Why not find a man and have Rodry come back from the dead? I *am* Lenore, and anyone who has been to court will know it. You will all know it, in time."

She looked out over them. "For now, I want you to think about the suffering that Ravin's rule is bringing."

"Nothing much is changing out here," the man in the crowd shouted back. Lenore could make him out now: a weasel-faced man with an underfed look to him. "I say all this is a matter for city folk."

"And will you be saying that when they come here?" Lenore said, raising her voice. "Will you be saying that when Ravin's soldiers demand your crops to feed his armies, while you starve? Will you be saying that when his laws mean harsh punishments for any who disobey his rule? When Quiet Men stalk the streets, looking out for traitors and taking anyone who even whispers the wrong words? When they take your daughters to be Ravin's playthings?"

"Like they kidnapped you, you mean?" the man shouted back. Now, Lenore could see her sister pushing her way through the crowd toward him. She could see the danger, wanted to call out to her sister, but she couldn't stop, couldn't lose the momentum of her speech. "This whole war's because of you," the man yelled.

"Yes, I was taken," Lenore said. "But if you think Ravin wouldn't have found another way, you're wrong. He is a cruel man, who will not stop until he holds all of your lives in his hand, or until *we* stop him."

"What can we hope to do?" That wasn't from the man who'd spoken before, but from a woman in the crowd, who looked to be standing there with her husband and children.

Lenore smiled at that. "You think you're too weak to stand up to an army, don't you? You think that you're nothing, that Ravin could brush you away with a flick of his hand. *I* thought that, when they took me, but it isn't true. We are all, every one of us, stronger than we think."

She gave them a moment for that to sink in. "There are more people in this kingdom than Ravin could hope to stand against, and his hold on it is tenuous at best. Those who side with him do so because they think there is no better choice. Well, we will give them a better choice. We will *be* that better choice. We will built an army together, and we will take back this kingdom from those who have stolen it!"

"Nonsense!" the man who had been heckling her shouted out, in the space where Lenore had half hoped that people would cheer. "Look at her. Just some girl. Even if she is the princess, what does that make her? An empty-headed noblewoman who never cared about any of us, and who threw herself into bed with the man who's Ravin's closest—"

"Don't talk about my sister like that!" Erin yelled as she reached him.

"Erin, don't!" Lenore shouted, but it was too late. She saw Erin's fist crack across the man's jaw, her knee come up into his stomach. He went down, and then Erin was kicking him, again and again, until Odd pulled her off him.

Now people were staring in horror at the violence. Lenore could practically feel the goodwill around her evaporating, and people started drifting off again, leaving the inn, some of them looking at her in disgust.

"No better than the invaders," the woman who'd spoken before said, as she and her family started to leave.

Lenore just stood there, not knowing what she could do to change their minds. She could only stand there, and stare.

She was still staring when Harris the miller walked through the dissipating crowd. He had a solidly built woman with him Lenore assumed was his wife, and he held out a hand, helping Lenore down from her perch on the table.

"I'm sorry," he said. "I know that didn't go the way that you wanted it to. Me and Tess here were impressed. And Nevis can run his mouth far too much sometimes."

"No," Lenore said. "I should have seen this coming. I should have stopped my sister."

"People are just shocked," the woman with him said. "When they stop to think about the things that you said, they'll start to realize that you were right."

"I hope so," Lenore said.

"They have to," Tess said. "Otherwise things will get worse. Oh, people used to complain about taxes and such under the old king, your father, but at least he was always fair. Those southerners will just take everything."

Lenore nodded. They'd already taken too many of the people she loved from her. "I hope they realize soon," she said. "I don't feel as though I'm doing much here."

"You've changed our minds," Harris said. "And I didn't think you'd manage that after the square earlier. Look, me and Tess have been talking and ... do you three have a place to stay?"

Lenore shook her head. She'd been planning to stay at the inn, or to set out on the road again.

"Then you'll stay with us," Tess said. "All of you. And maybe when people have had time to think, they'll start to come round."

Lenore hoped so. If they didn't, her fight back against Ravin's army was done before it had even begun.

CHAPTER SEVEN

"How's the water coming, Vars?"

Vars cursed as he struggled to lift the pail he was bringing from the pump behind Bethe's house, groaning as he started to carry it over.

She was waiting for him inside, working in the kitchen to make bread. Vars realized that it was something he'd never actually watched someone do before. It was a thing that servants did in the kitchens, well away from the sight of others.

The kitchen itself... well, it wasn't just a kitchen, because her room truly only had two rooms, this one and the one at the back for sleeping. Both were sparsely furnished with wooden furniture that had obviously all been made by the same hand. In the bedroom, there was one large bed, a chest for clothes, and a wardrobe. Bethe had laughed at Vars when he'd suggested that he should get the bed, or at the very least share it with her.

"Come help me knead this batch," Bethe said, and Vars bristled a little.

"I *was* a king, you know," he said, annoyance flashing through him.

"I know," Bethe said, with a faint smile, "and if you say it much louder, so will all my neighbors. Now come and actually be useful."

It had been the same almost constantly in the last few days. Vars had tried to remind her that he was important, someone to be respected, and each time she'd treated it as if he'd said something amusing and endearing.

Vars didn't know what to do with that. A part of him said that he should teach her some kind of lesson, that he should strike out at her to remind her that he was still more than someone like her could ever be.

He knew better, though, than to upset the one person who held his freedom in his hands like that.

So he kneaded the bread. It was a strange experience, pummeling the dough, working so hard to produce something as simple as bread. The effort of all this work was actually starting to make him breathe hard, and Vars found himself longing for soft beds and wine.

"Why … don't you … just … buy bread?" he demanded. What kind of person did all *this*?

"You think I have the money spare for that?" Bethe replied. "In any case, I make a little of the money I do make selling cakes and pastries. If people heard that I didn't even make my own bread, do you think they'd buy anything from me?"

It seemed strange to Vars that a few pastries here and there could make any kind of difference to someone's life. How could anyone be that poor? Yet it was undeniable that Bethe *was* poor, only just surviving from day to day. Even with that, she'd taken Vars in, saving him from people who would surely kill her if they found out. Vars didn't know whether to be amazed by the generosity of that or to think of it as something stupid beyond words.

To his surprise, a part of him found that he quite liked the peasant woman.

He managed a smile of his own. "I suppose it might bring in a bit more money if people know that I helped. You can say that your bread is by royal appointment."

Bethe laughed at that, and Vars had to admit that she was lovely when she laughed. She was lovely anyway, although to Vars's surprise and annoyance she hadn't shown any interest in him. He'd been used to women looking at him with at least respect, if not more, because of who he was.

Of course, that was the problem; he wasn't that person anymore. Even attempting to be would put him in danger. It was part of the reason he couldn't teach this woman the lesson she deserved.

With the bread kneaded, he put it to one side. "Can I rest yet," he demanded, "or are you going to think up some new torture for me?"

"You think we're done for the day?" Bethe countered.

Vars knew from experience that they weren't. Every day, there seemed to be a thousand irritating, backbreaking things to do, and never enough time to do them all. His body ached from the work of cleaning and cooking, fetching and carrying. He sighed with the anticipation of everything that was probably to come.

"Oh, don't be like that," Bethe said. "I'm just joking with you. Take a minute, drink some water. Then I'll need to take a trip down to the market, see if the soldiers have left any food for the rest of us. Pity you can't come with me; I could use an extra pair of hands to carry things."

They both knew the reasons why he couldn't. Even now, days after his escape from the castle, people might be looking for him. If they found him, Vars would be killed, and the fear of that had been enough to keep him within the house and its environs, even though a part of him was starting to see it as a prison as much as a safe haven.

He *wanted* to go further. Common sense told him that the best thing to do was to run, to get out of the city, to head for the furthest reaches of the kingdom, or even take a boat over the sea to one of the smaller islands. Even if he went to the Southern Kingdom, he might be safer than here. People might see that he was a northerner, but they wouldn't recognize Vars for who he truly was.

Of course, to do that, he would need to get out of the city. Every time Vars stepped outside, he felt as though there were eyes watching him from every window, although that might have something to do with the uniform that still represented his only clothes.

He wasn't sure right then whether the uniform was a help or a hindrance. To anyone who wasn't specifically looking for him, it probably meant that he was someone not to bother, but only while the uniform stayed clean enough that he could pass for a serving soldier. It was getting grubbier by the day, and that meant that Vars was starting to look more and more like a deserter, or some thief who had stolen from King Ravin's men. Even if no one recognized him, that could prove deadly.

"I'll need to get clothes," he said.

"And where am I going to get those?" Bethe said. "If you've got some coin tucked away, I could get you some from the market."

Vars shook his head. He didn't have any money. If he'd had money, he would have been able to buy some wine, for a start.

"Then—" A knock came at the door, and Vars saw Bethe's expression change sharply.

"Quick, in the back!"

Vars was already rushing for the door that led through to the back room. He'd done it enough times over the last few days, darting in there whenever someone had come to the door.

In the back room, there was a simple bed, a wardrobe of simple oak, and another chest of lighter wood, bound in iron and locked. There was a small chair, but Vars resisted the urge to sit on it, instead waiting and listening at the door. In the small space, he could pick up the words easily.

"That's fine, Moira. I'll have it made for you tomorrow."

"I've heard rumors that you've a new man around, Bethe. They're talking about a soldier."

Vars felt sick as he heard the words, feeling sure that the whole city had to know about him. He felt like running, slipping out the back of the dwelling and on into the city.

"People are gossiping about all the wrong things," Bethe replied. "That's my cousin, in from the villages, helping me out with a few things. I don't know where they're getting this 'soldier' business. I mean, he owns a red shirt..."

Vars was surprised at how easily the woman lied, and at the fact that she was willing to do it for him.

"Oh, can I meet him?" Moira said. Vars felt a fresh thrill of fear. Why wouldn't this woman just go?

"Well, he's not here right now, out at market."

"He wants to be careful, wearing red out there," Moira said. "People might think he's one of theirs. Hmm... is he good-looking?"

"*Moira!*" Vars could hear the shock there. "You're a married woman. And when I say cousin, I mean... not *exactly* a cousin."

"Well, if he's spoken for."

Vars frowned slightly at that. Bethe had been pleasant enough to him, but she hadn't seemed any more interested than that.

Thankfully, the visitor quickly left, and Vars was able to breathe a sigh of relief. He backed away from the door, making it to the chair before Bethe came through and looking up expectantly.

"I don't know why you do that," she said. "I'm sure you listen in."

"I ... might," Vars said. He didn't want to be too quick to admit it, because he didn't want to risk Bethe becoming angry with him and making him go.

"Well, I would too, if I were on the run. But that business about the shirt ... I've been thinking about this for a day or two now."

"Thinking about what?" Vars asked. Was she going to tell him that he had to go? *Where* would he go? What would he do?

Bethe went over to the chest, taking out a large iron key that she inserted into the lock. Vars heard the click as she turned it. She opened the chest and reached in, pulling out a light-colored peasant tunic, dark britches, and a wide leather belt. Vars stared at them in surprise as she took them out.

"These things were my husband's," Bethe said. "He was a kind man, he worked with wood. He was out in the street when the soldiers came into the city, and they ..."

"I'm so sorry," Vars said, and he was surprised to find that he *did* feel sympathy for Bethe. Normally, the fate of one peasant wouldn't have meant much to him, but now he could see the pain that it caused the woman in front of him, the grief lining her face.

"Edric would have wanted you to have his clothes," Bethe said. "He would have wanted to know that he was helping to keep someone safe. He was always such a generous man."

He sounded like the very opposite of everything that Vars was, and for a moment, Vars found himself feeling guilty that he'd been part of the reason so much horror had come down on the city. It was only a brief flash though, because in truth, what could anyone else have done, other than die?

"I'm grateful," Vars said, taking the clothes from Bethe gently. He cast off his stolen uniform, not caring that the shirt was slightly too big for him, or that the peasant woman was still there in front of him while he changed.

"You look better," Bethe said when he was done. "Now, we should probably burn that uniform."

Vars nodded. For a moment after he'd put on the clothes, he'd felt safe, but Bethe's words were a reminder that he was still in danger, could still be found and killed at any moment in this hovel, so far from anything in his former life.

So why, he wondered, did he feel content?

CHAPTER EIGHT

E rin sat outside, watching the blades of the windmill with her spear across her knee. A farmhouse sat beside it, and it lay on the edge of a small farm, also owned by Harris and his wife. That meant that there was enough space for her to be alone, at least for the moment.

That was good; the less time she spent with Odd right then, the better. She'd gone to him to have him teach her, but then he'd dared to hold her back out in the square where Ravin had murdered her mother.

If Odd hadn't held her back, Erin would have run across that square. She might have made it there in time to save her mother. She might at least have been able to cut down Ravin for what he'd done. The fact that she hadn't...that she'd just had to *stand* there...it made Erin's blood boil.

It wasn't enough though. All the anger in the world wouldn't be enough to hold back the grief that rose up behind it. Tears threatened to pour out of her, but even here, so far from anyone else, Erin refused to let them fall. She balled up her grief instead, burying it in her anger, using it to fuel her fury.

She took the cover from the head of her spear and stood, starting to move with it, practicing the blows and the parries that would be involved in a fight with a real opponent. As she moved, Erin imagined that opponent, seeing the way they moved, picturing every movement they might make.

At first, that opponent was an amorphous, shapeless thing, just an anonymous form to hold a sword. That wasn't enough, though, not to force Erin to move quickly, or to work through any of the anger that balled up in her head as she ducked and jumped, slashed and stabbed.

Slowly, her imaginary opponent took on the features of King Ravin, and Erin sped up, thinking of all the ways that she might strike at him. In her mind, she killed him a hundred times, spearing him through the heart or the throat, slashing the blade of her weapon across the arteries of the arm or the leg. Her spear slashed through the air outside the windmill, spinning in an imitation of its blades. Erin imagined all the ways that fight might go, all the ways that she might bring down the man who had caused her family so much misery.

Slowly, the face of her opponent shifted again, and Erin found herself facing up to the image of Odd, standing there with that effortless calm of his, that look that seemed to treat her efforts as those of a child. Erin sped up again, striking and defending, blisteringly fast now as she leapt and span, sending her spear out toward the face as someone approached.

Erin barely held the weapon back in time to keep it from killing Tess, the miller's wife. Erin lowered the spear and stared at the woman, who was holding a trencher on which sat a bowl of stew and some bread.

"I thought... I thought you would want something to eat," she said. She sounded a little afraid, as if worried that the fury inside Erin would spill out over her to consume her.

"Thank you," Erin said. She sheathed the long blade of her half spear.

"That's an unusual weapon," the other woman said.

"A swordmaster picked it out for me," Erin replied. "He said it suited me more than a longsword. I'm going to plunge it into Ravin's heart one day."

She didn't mention the other figure she'd been thinking of fighting. She ate, instead, and Tess stayed with her while she did.

"Your sister is lucky to have you to protect her," Tess said.

Erin shrugged. "What she really needs is an army."

"Well, there might be a beginning on that front at least," Tess said. "The others wanted me to fetch you back to the house. I just thought I'd give you time to finish your food first."

"What do you mean, 'a beginning'?" Erin asked.

"Come and see," Tess said.

She led the way back up to the farmhouse, and Erin found Lenore and Odd in front of it. Lenore stood there like a general commanding an army, while Odd seemed to have brought his monk's robes with him, because he was back in them, leaning on his sheathed sword, his noble clothes gone now.

Along with them, there were what looked to be around half a dozen men. A couple had swords that were obviously left over from military service by themselves or their fathers, while the others held agricultural implements, axes and sickles, even a scythe.

"Erin!" Lenore called out as she got closer. She looked so happy in that moment that someone had come, someone had responded to her speech. Erin was happy for her, but at the same time, she could see just what a small beginning it was. Armies needed thousands of men, not six.

"They came because they heard me at the inn," Lenore explained. "Thom and Kurt have served as soldiers before, and the others are willing to learn."

"They will have a lot to learn," Odd said, and Erin flashed him a hard look, even though it was more or less what she'd been thinking.

"It's a start," she said.

"And we'll get more," Lenore said. "Harris and Tess are going to let us use their farm for all who come to me. We'll train here, and we'll produce a fighting force that can actually strike at Ravin."

Erin tried to imagine these men up against the Southern Kingdom's soldiers. They would need a lot of training.

Lenore beckoned Erin and Odd off to one side, going into the farmhouse, away from the men who were just starting to practice with their weapons. Harris and Tess went with them.

"There's another part to this," Lenore said, once they were safely inside, ensconced in front of a fire that warmed the large, stone-walled kitchen. "Those men are a start, and there will be more, but if we're going to win, we need real fighting men on our side. We need the nobles."

"I'm not sure if you'd want Lord Carrick," Harris said. "He's … a hard man. Part of the reason people didn't react to your speech about the new emperor making things worse is that Lord Carrick already taxes us hard."

"Barely leaves folk enough to live," Tess agreed.

"He's the lord around here?" Lenore asked. "I think I heard you say his name out on the village green."

"He is," Harris said. "Lives in the big castle southeast of here. He sends his men out to hang thieves and make sure everyone knows who owns this place."

To Erin, he sounded no different to half the lords in the kingdom. Her father had tried to make sure that he had good men around him, but no one held onto their lands unless they were tough enough to deal with bandits or uprisings. Still, she could see Lenore thinking it over. Even as she did so, Erin was having her own thoughts.

"I think I've heard of this Carrick," Odd said. "He is as they say, a tough man, maybe even a cruel one. But he used to be loyal to the crown, when I was ... well, before I was this."

Was he that ashamed of who he'd been? Was he that scared of the anger that had been in him? For Erin, the anger was the only thing keeping her moving right then.

Lenore made a decision.

"Then we will need to travel to see him," she said. "I will speak with him, and do everything I can to gain his support. If I can remind him of his loyalty, then maybe we'll have his men at our disposal."

"It will still only be one lord," Erin pointed out.

Her sister nodded. "I know, but we have to start somewhere with the lords, just as we do with gathering an army. Once we get one lord, others will follow."

"No one wants to be the first to do anything," Odd agreed. "The abbot used to say that a dam will stand unblemished for years, but once the first trickle appears, it is only a matter of time before the flood."

Erin wasn't sure if that was supposed to pass for wisdom, but to her, it was simply irritating. Odd might be wearing a monk's robes, but there was nothing holy about him, whatever he pretended.

"While we go, people can continue to come here," Lenore said. "It will give them a place to gather, and one where they can start to train." She looked over to Harris and Tess. "If that's all right with both of you? I don't want to put you in danger."

"We wouldn't have offered if we weren't willing to take the risk," Tess said. "We'll let people gather here, and they can use the fields to practice, but I'm not sure if they'll know what to do when there are only a few real soldiers."

Erin saw her chance. "I'll stay."

Lenore glanced over at her. "You don't want to come?"

"You'll have Odd with you to protect you," Erin said. She hoped that she could trust him to do at least that much. He was a good fighter, whatever else he was. "And I don't need to be there, begging some noble for his favor."

She could see Lenore considering it, and Erin knew why. She was probably thinking about how much simpler another speech would be without Erin attacking someone in the middle of it.

"I could start to train people as they come," Erin said. "I know the Knights of the Spur threw me out, but I still trained with them."

Lenore still didn't look convinced.

"There should be at least one of the two of us here," Erin said. "Just so that people know that this is real. Besides, this is the place where I can do the most good. You ... you have a knack for talking to people, you were brought up to deal with courtiers and nobles. Well, this is what *I'm* good at."

Finally, Lenore nodded. "If you're sure."

"I'm sure," Erin said. She'd never been more certain of anything in her life. It had nothing to do with the prospect of more farmers, though. She had her own plan, and if she did this right, it would end all this, once and for all.

CHAPTER NINE

A urelle led the way as she and the others headed for Royalsport. She was the one who was best placed to spot trouble coming, and probably the one with the best chance of killing anyone who came at them in an ambush.

Renard and Orianne followed a couple of paces behind, Renard leaning on the royal maid servant for support. Renard looked frail by now, the life sucked out of him, his hair bleached to something almost white, so that Aurelle could barely tell by looking that it had once been red like hers. His muscular frame was bent, moving slowly, looking like it was held up only by Orianne's efforts, and by the stick wedged under his arm.

For her part, Orianne looked worn by her ordeal at the hands of Finnal's men, but grateful to still be alive. She was bruised but beautiful, her dark hair tied back out of the way, showing the darkening on her cheek where someone had hit her. There was a determined set to her features as she helped Renard, her eyes intent on the prospect of Royalsport ahead and what might happen there.

Aurelle imagined that her own expression would look pretty similar right then. She had to get back to Royalsport, because there were men there who needed to die. Finnal and his father, Duke Viris, would pay for what they'd done, for Greave's death and for all the manipulations that had gone on before it. The thought of getting that revenge spurred her to walk faster, eager to be there.

"Not too fast," Renard said. "I can't keep up."

Maybe once, Aurelle would have abandoned him, because the mission had always come before anything; before friendship, before kindness, before any sense of what was right. With Greave though, she'd seen that *some* things at least *did* matter more. She was going to get to Royalsport, but the others were too.

Aurelle could see it ahead now, with its walls and its bridges, its river system that served to both defend it and connect it to the world. Her eyes took in the poorer houses beyond the walls, the people on the roads leading in and out, and the forms of the tallest buildings inside the city standing out above the rest. The towers of the House of Scholars were always the easiest to see, and the bulk of the castle dominated the rest, but her eyes focused more on the brightness of the House of Sighs, standing out over the city's entertainment district. That was their destination.

"Not far now," she said to the others.

Even as Aurelle said it, though, her eyes took in other things. Because she'd been trained to look out for potential threats, she automatically took in the presence of the guards at the gates, and the soldiers who moved among the people outside the city, overseeing their activities.

She looked around to explain the dangers to the other two, but saw that they were already looking. It was easy to forget that, whatever his current state, Renard was meant to be a master thief, while Orianne had spent her share of time at the House of Sighs.

"We'll need to find a way in," she said.

"Ordinarily, I'd suggest climbing the walls," Renard said, and then gestured to his crutch. "Today though, I'd rather find something less ... energetic."

"A smuggler's way in?" Orianne suggested.

Ordinarily, it might have been a good idea, but Aurelle could see the way the Southern Kingdom's troops had things under their gaze.

"My guess is that by now they'll be watching all the hidden routes closely," she said. "If we don't know which ones are safe, there's too much of a risk of running into patrols, and then they'll ask questions we don't have answers for."

"So how do we do it, then?" Orianne asked. "We *need* to get inside the city."

"I think we just walk in the front gate," Aurelle said. "It will be less suspicious that way. We just need a good cover story."

"That part's easy enough," Renard said. "We tell them that we're heading for the House of Sighs."

Aurelle frowned at him. "You want to cunningly lie to the guards by telling them the truth? Exactly how good a thief were you?"

"I was, and remain, the best," Renard said with a hint of pride. It might have been more convincing if he hadn't needed Orianne to hold him up. "Look at the people going in. Some of them look desperate."

"A lot of them will *be* desperate," Orianne said, beside him. "So soon after an invasion, they won't have much."

"So we play on that," Renard said. "You're both too well dressed to pass for peasant folk, and in this state, I can hardly say that I'm coming into the city to work. We've nothing we can pretend to be selling, so that's out. But if we hint that you're both going to seek work in the House of Sighs..."

Aurelle nodded; it might work. Some of the best lies were those that contained a hint of the truth, and this one would mean that no one would question the direction they headed in. In any case, they'd taught her that lies that seemed sufficiently personal, or embarrassing, had less chance of being questioned.

"All right," she said. "We'll do it."

"There's still the question of what Renard's doing with us," Orianne said.

"It's fine," Aurelle said. "I have it worked out."

The others seemed to take her at her word, and they headed for the gates. They didn't push through the crowds waiting for entrance, or at least, they didn't do it overtly. Aurelle didn't want to cause trouble that might attract too much scrutiny. At the same time, she made sure that she and the others kept moving forward. The less time they spent in one place, the less chance there was of anything going wrong.

As they got closer, Aurelle looked at what waited for them at the gates. There were a couple of guards there, along with another man who might have been an officer, and a man sitting at a table, apparently writing down names and purposes in visiting the city. She'd been confident before of their plan, yet now, nervousness built inside her with every step, imagining all the ways that this might go wrong. There was no way to pull back now though. People who started to back away when faced with guards were always the ones those guards paid the most attention to.

"Name?" the man at the desk demanded.

Renard was there in that moment, putting on a voice so old and cracked that... well, that it matched the rest of him.

"I'm Irrien," he said. "These here are my daughters, Edna and Hilda. We're here because times are hard, and... well..."

"And you thought a couple of pretty young women might make you enough to get by at the House of Sighs?" the officer said, moving in close. His hand reached out for Aurelle's hair, and Aurelle let a knife fall from her sleeve into her palm, just so that she could feel the weight of it.

"They're fine enough, I suppose," the officer said. "And that gets them in. But why should I let you in? What are *you* going to do in the city?"

"Oh, I can sing a little," Renard said. "Play the lute a bit. Thought I'd entertain folk at the House."

"Then sing," the officer said. "My men could always use a bit of entertainment. And when we hear you're no good, you can crawl back to whatever hole you crawled out of, while the women go in."

Aurelle tensed. This wasn't going the way she'd hoped.

"Or *they* could entertain us," the officer said. Now Aurelle was sure that she was going to have to kill him. She would have to pick her moment, and then they would all have to run, except that there was no way that Renard could run.

Then Renard did the one thing Aurelle hadn't expected, and started to sing. He did it in a low, full voice, singing a bawdy song that almost made Aurelle blush to hear it. It seemed to catch the officer by surprise, but then the man smiled. One of the soldiers there even started to tap his foot in time with it.

"All right," the officer said. "We can't hang around here listening to you all day. Get inside."

Aurelle breathed a sigh of relief as they made their way through the gates.

"I didn't know you could sing like that," she said.

"I am *famed* for my ability to perform," Renard said. "Although usually it's because I get thrown out of inns halfway through."

He gave a hacking cough, and it was a reminder to Aurelle of just how urgently they needed to keep going.

They headed through the city, and Aurelle could see just how much had changed, but also how much had stayed the same. There were soldiers in Ravin's red and purple on too many of the streets, moving in patrols, watching over everything that took place there. There were patches of the city where people worked in gangs under their control, rebuilding houses or other buildings. Carts appeared to be moving goods toward the edges, again controlled by the soldiers.

At the same time, shops were open, and people were out in the streets. The House of Weapons still had smoke from its forges billowing in the sky, and the noise of the city was still bustling and loud.

It made it at least straightforward for them to make their way over the city, crossing the bridges with the rest of the crowds, heading for the entertainment district. When they reached the square where the House of Sighs sat, Aurelle was a little surprised by the number of people there, but then she realized that she shouldn't be. The story that she'd spun for the guards had worked so well because it was true for plenty of other people. They crowded in front of the door, so that Aurelle knew it would be hard to get in that way.

Thankfully, Aurelle knew where all the small side doors were, for the more discreet clients. She led the way around to one, knocking in a sequence that she hoped hadn't been changed since she left.

The woman who opened it was muscled and dangerous looking. Aurelle recognized Sula, and it seemed that the other woman recognized her.

"You ... you're alive."

Aurelle nodded. "And I've come with friends. Is Meredith here? Will she see us?"

"She's just back from the castle, but for you, I think she'll see you."

She led the way through the House of Sighs, and Aurelle was surprised by how much she'd missed the silk screens and painted walls of the place. She took them to Meredith's office, where the mistress of the House of Sighs was waiting, looking drawn from her efforts.

Even so, she smiled as she looked up and saw them.

"Aurelle, Orianne, you're safe!" She stood, moving to Aurelle and hugging her. She stepped back and stared at her. A note of realization came into her expression. "And you're just in time. I think ... I think you just made a plan possible that might save us all."

CHAPTER TEN

W hen Devin arrived on the edges of Royalsport, he could see the things that were different almost instantly, and the pain of seeing it flooded through him. He could see the damaged houses around the edges, the spaces where buildings should have been. Each one was like a missing piece of himself.

Sigil padded by his side, the wolf looking out over Royalsport as if not able to comprehend the scope of such a large human place. Devin reached down to touch his fur, brushing the strange mark in the shape of a mystical rune that grew there. Instantly, Devin felt a connection to the magic around him.

He knew he probably didn't look the way he had when he'd left. His hair was still dark, but now it had grown longer than it had been. He still had his share of small scars and burn marks from the forge fires of the House of Weapons, but now they'd been joined by scars from the battles needed to find all the pieces of the unfinished sword. That was now all but finished, the blade and tang wrapped in a bundle across Devin's back.

Devin *felt* different, too. So much had happened since he'd left. He'd seen friends die, and had learned more about the way magic worked than he could have imagined. Yet one thing remained the same: what he felt for Lenore. He needed to find her, find out what was going on in Royalsport, work out what he was going to do next.

He looked down at Sigil.

"I guess we'd be pretty conspicuous walking around the city together," he said. "We need to find somewhere safe I can leave you for a little while."

There was only one place outside of the walls that Devin could think of: his parents' house. At least, the house of the people he'd thought of as his parents for so long. Devin set off in the direction of it, avoiding the main streets, heading for the poor part of town where it sat. He just hoped that they would be willing to open the door to him. After the last time he'd been there, it wasn't certain.

The street on which the house stood was quiet, and Devin stood there, just staring at the house for a moment. It seemed so much smaller now than it had before, or maybe it was just that he'd spent so much time in so many different places. A small house in a poor district of the city somehow didn't seem like enough anymore.

Devin went to it anyway, knocking on the door tentatively. There was no reply.

"Mother, Father?" he called out. "It's me, Devin."

Still, there was no answer, and Devin tried the door. He still had his key, and it swung open at his touch, revealing the interior of the house. It was empty, with no sign that his parents were there, and no sign that they had been there for some time. A layer of dust stood on everything, in a way that it wouldn't if there had been anyone to sweep it away. Worry rose in Devin. His parents, and he couldn't help thinking of them like that, even now, had thrown him out, but he still cared about them, and still wanted to be sure that they were all right.

It felt wrong being here without them, but Devin wasn't sure what other option he had. He went into the kitchen, finding scraps of meat and setting them in a bowl.

"I need you to stay here until I get back," he said to Sigil. He didn't know if the wolf could understand him or not, but Devin said it all the same. "I need to go into the city. I need to find out what's happening here."

The wolf lay down, licking at the bowl, and Devin took that as his cue to leave. From his house, he headed toward the House of Weapons, reasoning that there was no chance of him getting into the castle now, but that at least he might be able to find someone in the House who could tell him exactly how things sat in the city.

He started to make his way along the streets, toward the interior of the city. There were guards on the city gate, but as soon as Devin mentioned the House of Weapons, they stood back to let him pass. Apparently, Ravin's men needed weaponry as much as everyone else. He kept the unfinished sword wrapped up though. He didn't want anyone seeing it and thinking that he was there to fight.

How many times had Devin walked the path to the House of Weapons in his life? From the moment he'd gotten a job there as an apprentice to the day they'd made him leave, he'd walked this route almost every morning, rain or shine. It was as familiar to him as the contours of his own hands, yet now he could see the fear in people's faces as he passed, and the damage to the city from the invasion.

Devin could see the House of Weapons ahead, towering over the rest of it, the orange light of its fires glowing from its windows while dark smoke came from its chimneys. Devin stood there, trying to work out the best way inside. Perhaps he could tell them the truth: that he had been a smith there. Perhaps they would assume he was looking for work and let him in.

Devin was still contemplating it when he saw a large shape heading in the direction of the House. He recognized Nem immediately, the boy's simple, open face staring up at the place they'd both worked as he went toward it.

"Nem?" he called out, and the boy stopped, turning toward him.

"Devin?" Nem's expression split in a smile. "I thought you were dead like the others!"

"I'm all right," Devin assured him. "But what happened here, Nem?"

"The southerners invaded," Nem said, as if it were obvious. He looked sad for a moment. "Gund is dead. Lots of people are dead."

Devin winced at the news that the smith who had run his section of the forge was dead.

"Tell me all of it," Devin said. "I've been … out of the city. I don't know what's going on."

"They invaded," Nem said again, as if that covered it. He'd never been the brightest. "They came in the city when the streams were low, and they tried to take it. They say the wizard tried to hold them back by making the streams run fast, but it wasn't enough. He disappeared. Just vanished. No one knows where he went."

Devin wasn't surprised by that part. If Master Grey decided to lose himself, no one else was going to be able to find him.

"What happened then?" he asked.

"The soldiers ... there were soldiers everywhere. They killed people, I saw them, in the street ..."

"It's all right, Nem," Devin said, putting a hand on the boy's shoulder.

"It's not. They killed lots of people. Gund, a lot of other smiths, the weapon masters. Even Wendros."

Devin winced again. He hadn't known Wendros well, and the man had tried to talk him out of becoming a swordsman, but even so, Devin had respected the swordmaster.

"Have you heard anything about my parents?" Devin asked, knowing he had to at least try to find answers.

Nem shook his head. "A lot of people were killed though. A lot of people."

There was a haunted look in the boy's eyes as he said it that suggested he'd seen a lot of painful things the night King Ravin's people had invaded.

Devin's next question was one that a part of him didn't want to ask, because he was afraid of hearing the answer. Even so, he knew that he couldn't leave it be. He had to know.

"What about ... what about Princess Lenore?" he asked.

Nem shook his head. "They say King Ravin killed all of them, all the royal folk. King Vars let them into the castle. He killed Queen Aethe out in the big square, and he had his Quiet Men kill the others. Everyone says so, but quiet, so no one bad hears them."

"Lenore ... Lenore's dead?" Devin said. He stared at his friend. He couldn't believe it. Nem had to be wrong, or lying, or ... but that was the problem when it came to Nem; he could no more lie to someone than he could recite fine poetry or read beyond the letters of his name. He could craft the finest metalwork, but he couldn't even begin to craft a lie.

That meant ... that meant that Devin was too late.

Grief poured over him. He hadn't been there when Master Grey made the rivers rise, hadn't seen the torrents of water that had come rushing through the city, but Devin felt as though he understood then what it must have been like to stand in front of them and be overwhelmed.

The pain was absolute, and it was all that he could do to keep standing. All the other losses were bad enough, friends and people he'd known, with his parents missing somewhere in the violence. Even after they'd thrown him out, Devin could feel the hurt of that.

The loss of Lenore was worse than all of it. Devin felt as though he was collapsing in on himself, all the strength going out of him, until it seemed that he might crumple and fall right there in the street. He leaned back against the nearest building, a choking sob coming from him in spite of his best efforts to stop it.

He didn't remember saying goodbye to Nem. He didn't remember walking back along the route toward his parents' house. His feet must have done it numbly, from pure memory, because the next time he was able to look through the blinding haze of his grief was when he was opening the door.

Sigil was there to meet him, and Devin wrapped his arms around the wolf, sitting there on the floor, staring out at the far wall while tears fell from his eyes.

"I was too late, boy. I was too late."

He'd come here to save Lenore, and now ... now that chance was gone. He'd stopped his work on the Unfinished Sword to come here, and he'd still been too late. It sat there by the far wall, still wrapped up, but for now, Devin hurt too much to even think about it.

CHAPTER ELEVEN

The room they gave Renard at the House of Sighs was … red. Very red. The sheets were red, the drapes were red, even the furniture was made of wood of such a deep hue it could have been stained in blood. Some flicker of memory stirred inside Renard, so that he was sure he had been in it before, but sorting through all his memories of the House of Sighs was … complicated, and Renard didn't have the attention to spare, right then.

He found himself focusing instead on the feeling of the amulet by his side, slowly draining the life from him, even now. Renard sat, looking around the room. This was one occasion when maybe memory was actually useful, rather than something to be pushed away, out of embarrassment.

He *did* remember this room. He'd been here before, and that meant … he walked over to a spot in the corner, lifting the edge of a delicately embroidered rug and finding a place where his knife could dig into the space between two floorboards.

As weak as he was, it was an effort to pry up the one that was loose, revealing the space beneath. There was a box there, made of a mixture of copper and gold that fit together the way marquetry might in a wooden box. Renard caressed it; he could still remember the moment when he'd stolen it. Of course, having to leave it here had been … less than ideal, but right now, it presented an opportunity.

He touched the box in one place, then another, pushing gently so that he wouldn't trigger any of the needles built into it. The top unfolded like a flower blooming, revealing an open space in which sat a ring, a smooth carved ruby, and a few coins of indeterminate value.

Renard took those out on general principles, but also so that he could make space. He set the amulet in the box and teased the sections back together. They clicked into place, and Renard set the box back under the floorboard, putting the board back in place and setting the rug on top of it.

He went back to the bed, the effort even of that much having tired him. Yet Renard could feel his strength start to flow back into him, little by little, the way it had when he'd briefly given the amulet to the merchant.

He *could* just leave it there. He could get up from this bed, walk out of the House of Sighs, and never come back. He could lose himself, and this time it wouldn't be like Geertstown, because the amulet wouldn't be out there in the open, where anyone could just grab it.

But the Hidden would still be coming for it, and any dragons who came close enough to sense it. They would all destroy the House of Sighs without a thought in order to get at it, and as much as Renard wanted to say that had nothing to do with him, he knew that it did.

Life would be so much easier without a conscience.

He was still contemplating when he'd managed to grow one of *those* when the door to his very red room opened and Meredith walked in.

"I thought it was you," she said, looking him over. "I wasn't sure, but the others don't know not to use your name. They don't know that it's banned here."

"It's good to see you too, Meredith," Renard said, sitting up. He was halfway through the movement when Meredith pressed a slender blade to his neck. "You're looking as lovely as ever."

"You're not," she replied. "Although you're looking better than you did when you walked in."

"Soon you won't be able to keep your hands off me," Renard said.

She increased the pressure on the knife, just a fraction. "There were reasons you were told never to come back here, Renard. After what you did—"

"It was a long time ago," Renard protested, raising his hands.

"Not long enough," Meredith snapped back. At least she took the knife away from his throat.

"I didn't *want* to come back," Renard said. "I had to. I need to find the king's sorcerer."

"There are a lot of people looking for him right now," Meredith said. "He's gone."

Renard swore, long and loud. Meredith stared at him while he did it, then laughed.

"I'd forgotten what you were like when you were disappointed. It must have been really important for you to find him, if you're prepared to come back *here*."

"It was," Renard said. "Life or death."

Meredith looked at him as if trying to gauge him. She'd always been good at seeing through his lies. What she saw there now must have caught her by surprise, because her eyes widened slightly.

"All right," she said. "But I should still throw you out."

"Would you be so cruel?" Renard said. He tried his most winning smile. "To me, of all people?"

He heard her sigh. "Maybe we can find some use for you. Come with me. I'm meeting with the others in the orangery, but I wanted to decide whether I was going to kill you before I let you join that meeting."

"I suppose I should be honored," Renard said, as Meredith led the way. "Especially when you remembered the old room, and what—"

"Mention any of that in front of people, and I *will* kill you," Meredith said, without looking back.

She led the way to a room at the top of the House of Sighs, where a glass roof provided light for citrus trees to thrive, and chairs had been set out among them. Aurelle and Orianne sat there already, and both looked significantly less road-worn than they had. Aurelle had picked out a dark outfit of gray and black, complete with kidskin gloves and boots. Orianne was wearing a fresh dress of green velvet, elegant and simple in its beauty, the bruises on her face covered by makeup now.

"You've all been through a lot," Meredith said, as Renard took one of the seats there, "but the whole city, the entire *kingdom*, has been. We need to act if we're going to stop all of this."

"You have a plan," Renard guessed, because he'd never known Meredith to be without a plan.

She nodded. "But I'll need your help. People have talked about killing Ravin, or his allies, or whoever, but it's not *enough*."

"Killing someone usually stops them," Aurelle pointed out. Renard already knew that she had someone in mind, because she'd told him as much out on the road.

"And then what?" Meredith countered. "We need to create the conditions so that, when Ravin falls, things actually change. We can't just let it be about killing one man; we need to destabilize the whole regime, and do it without being seen."

"I already *have* a task here, Meredith," Aurelle said. "The men responsible for Greave's death have to pay."

"And they will," Meredith said. "But for now, killing Duke Viris or his son would be ... inconvenient."

"It's not about what's *convenient*!" Aurelle snapped. "It's about what's right!"

"And what's right about leaving the city in the southerners' hands?" Meredith demanded.

Renard sighed. "Meredith's right, Aurelle. I never thought I'd hear myself say this, but sometimes you have to put what you want aside for the greater good."

"And *I* definitely never thought I would hear Renard the thief say something like that," Meredith said. "But he's right; this is bigger than all of us. We're each placed to shift things in the city, but we have to do our parts, or it won't work."

Aurelle looked to Renard as if she might be about to stand and walk out, but she didn't.

"What do you need us to do?" she asked, in a careful voice, one that still hadn't fully agreed to anything yet. Renard could tell just how important her revenge was to her.

"We need to start to pry nobles away from Ravin's side," Meredith said. "But without it being obvious. We need to listen, and gather information. When we hear dissatisfaction, we need to make the smallest moves to fan the flames. I ... already have access to the castle, so I will start to whisper to those among his entourage who are dissatisfied, and I will listen out for rumors. Men like that always have a thousand small feuds with one another. Ravin thinks he has me contained and controlled, but I will find a way to use it." She looked over to Orianne. "You can't be seen by those loyal to Ravin, but people will know you as Princess Lenore's maid. That means you can go to the few remaining loyal to King Godwin and his family, persuading them to work with us, setting up ways for them to do it quietly."

Renard thought that was a good idea, although he wasn't sure how openly most of them would be able to act.

"Aurelle," Meredith said. "I need you to do something harder. I need you to go to Finnal and his father, and I need you to tell them that you succeeded in your mission. I know how much you want to kill them, I *know* how hard it can be to be around someone you've sworn to put a blade in ..." Did she give Renard a quick glance in that moment? "... but you're our best chance to get someone where they can start to sow dissent with the ones who are loyal to Ravin."

To Renard's eye, Aurelle didn't look happy about it, but even so, she nodded.

"All right, I'll do it. When this is done though ..."

"When it's done, they'll be dead," Meredith promised her.

There was only one part of her plan that Meredith hadn't articulated yet, and it was the part Renard most wanted to hear.

"What about me?" he said. "If you're bringing me into this, you must have something in mind for me."

"In time, yes," Meredith said. "When you're recovered enough to be of any use. For now, though, I have a task for you that I suspect will prove to be the most difficult of your life."

"What?" Renard demanded. He thought of all the dangers he'd faced in the preceding days, from Lord Carrick's executioner to the Hidden, being chased by dragons to the lingering threat of the amulet. What could possibly be so difficult compared with all of that?

"I need you to stay here and stay out of trouble," Meredith said. "And if your last visit is anything to go by, that's going to be more difficult than every other element of this put together."

CHAPTER TWELVE

For so much of his life, Odd hadn't really cared about anything beyond himself. When he'd been younger, and a rising nobleman, everything had been about his own importance, his own growing skills with the blade. When he'd been a knight, it had been about his anger, the fury within him driving away even distinctions regarding who was friend or foe. Even when he'd been a monk, it had been about improving himself, changing himself, saving himself.

Now, he had Lenore to protect, and as they walked together along the route that would take them to Lord Carrick's castle, Odd was taking that duty seriously. He looked at the path ahead, trying to pick out any dangers, then scanned the surrounding fields in case there were foes hidden in them. His eyes fell on a man leading a donkey through some tall grass, resting on him for long moments as he tried to work out if the man was a threat.

"You can relax, Odd," Lenore said. "I know that if there is a threat, you'll protect me."

"With my life, if needed," Odd promised her.

Lenore shook her head. "I don't want you dying for me. I want you alive to fight for me. You and Erin are both essential to what's coming."

Odd winced at the sound of the younger princess's name. The tension between him and his former student had been there for days, and Odd wasn't sure what to do about any of it.

"What is it between you and her at the moment?" Lenore asked, continuing to walk down the road.

"It's nothing," Odd said, but Lenore didn't let him get away with that.

"A moment ago, you said that you would willingly die for me, but now you aren't prepared to tell me the truth?" she said.

Odd sighed, because he knew that Lenore was correct. If she was his ruler, then he owed it to her to be honest about this.

"I worry about Erin," he said. "I have seen anger like hers before, and far too often, it was when I looked into a mirror."

"She has lost a lot," Lenore said, while they walked along by a length of dry stone wall.

"She has, as have you, but you have dealt with it in different ways," Odd said. He closed his eyes for a moment. "I have always had anger in me, but it wasn't always an all-consuming thing. It wasn't always the battle rage that it became."

Lenore stopped, perching on a section of the wall and giving Odd her full attention. "Then what happened, Odd? What made you what you were?"

As young as she was compared to him, it still made Odd feel confident about her skills as a leader. Here she was, breaking off her trip to gain allies, simply because one of her followers seemed to need it.

"When I was a young man, my father died in a duel," Odd said. "I had already fought in battles, but that moment was like oil thrown atop burning kindling. Even though I didn't like my father, I sought out the man who had killed him, and the anger as I cut him down ... it was like a doorway I could walk through, but not walk back from. Every moment after that, the anger was waiting under the surface, because it never felt like enough. Killing that one man had been too simple, and facing up to the pain of it all was too much. It was easier to keep killing."

It wasn't something he usually talked about. He'd told people the rest before, about the Knights of the Spur, and how they'd seen him as useful, even about the villagers he'd slaughtered in the uprising, but this part he usually held for himself.

"You came through it though," Lenore said.

"Eventually," Odd agreed. "But a great many people suffered along the ..." He paused as a scent caught his nose: blade oil and sweat, close and caught on the wind. "Wait, do you smell that?"

He leapt past the princess, vaulting the wall and jumping into the wheat of the field beyond. Odd drew his sword in one smooth movement, holding it balanced and poised at head level, point out toward whatever threat would come, weight shifted back, ready to spring forward. He could feel his focus growing pin sharp, could feel the beating of his heart within his chest.

Even as he did so, a trio of men rose out of the field, dressed in ragged clothes. One looked as though he had once been a villager, while others seemed like former soldiers. All three carried weapons. The first of them to reach Odd swung an axe at his head, but Odd was already beating aside the blow, countering with a diagonal cut that hacked the man down.

Another came in with a sword and Odd stepped in to meet him, blade ringing against blade as the two met. Odd let go of his sword's grip with his left hand, grabbing at the man's wrist as he stepped to the side and twisted his blade free of the bind. He brought the longsword around in another deadly arc, this time meeting with the base of the man's neck.

He lowered his sword now in front of him, like a boar hunting for acorns. Then, as the third man came at him, Odd shifted back, bringing his sword up like the questing tusks of that boar. His opponent's sword stroke whistled past him. His own thrust didn't miss.

Even as the last of the bandits fell, Odd saw more rustling among the wheat, and hidden men rose up out of it. There had to be twenty of them, clutching an assortment of weapons, and even if he'd been able to deal with the first three quickly, Odd knew that this many would be too much for him. No man, however deadly, could hope to fight more than a few foes at once and live.

Right then, though, it wasn't about him living.

"Run, Princess!" Odd called. "I will hold them for as long as I can!"

"No," Lenore insisted. "I will not leave you to die."

Odd knew that she was serious, that she would not run while he stood. His only hope was to give her a reason to run, and the only way to do that was to throw himself forward into the fray.

Odd tensed himself to do exactly that. He thought about his life, all the failures of it, all the people he'd killed. There would be more still in the moments before he died, because he could not imagine going to the grave without at least taking a few of them with him. He thought of the family he'd lost, the friends who had turned out not to be friends once they'd seen the kind of man he was. He thought of the faces of people who had died screaming their hatred of him, and even after so many, he could still make out each one.

Odd's grip tightened on his longsword.

"Wait," Lenore said, and then raised her voice. "Wait, Odd. I command it."

There was such a note of authority in her voice that Odd froze in place in spite of himself. He saw Lenore walk in front of him, into the field, among the fallen.

"You don't get to throw your life away for me," Lenore said to him, and Odd felt a note of shame in that moment so great that he fell to one knee.

"Forgive me, my queen," he said.

Lenore touched his shoulder lightly, drawing him to his feet. She turned to the others there. "You men. You used to live in the villages around here, didn't you? Or you used to fight in the king's armies?"

"What's it to you?" one of them called back.

"You used to have lives," Lenore said. "You used to have people you loved, and places where you felt safe. My guess is that when the invasion came, you lost those. For the soldiers, either you fought for the king, and you became wanted men, or you ran when you should have held, and you became hated men."

Odd saw her point to one of the ones dressed like a villager, and he didn't think it was a coincidence that it was the one who was closest, the one Odd was already working out how to cut down if he got too near.

"For the villagers, it would have been homes taken, crops seized, loved ones cut down. Either you fought, and you became outlaws, or you didn't fight, and those you loved looked at you with pity and with shame, because you didn't do enough to protect them. What did they take from *you*?"

"They killed my brother," the man said. "Would have killed me, but I ran."

"They killed my brother too," Lenore said. "While he was in the Southern Kingdom, saving me. I ran, but I am *done* with running. I am Princess Lenore of the Northern Kingdom, and I plan to take back what is mine."

The words rang out over the field, and they seemed to stun the men into silence. Odd had been beside many leaders over the years, but none of them had managed to get men to stare at them the way they did at Lenore in that moment.

"You could come at me now," she said. "And if you do, I'm sure my protector knight will cut many of you down before you finally kill us. You could run, and wait for the next traveler. Or you could join me. You are fighting men, but you have forgotten what you're fighting for. Don't fight to take a few coins from the weak; fight to take a whole kingdom back from those who have already stolen it. Will you join me? Will you?"

Even after that, Odd half expected them to charge. When the first man came forward, Odd tensed to strike him down, but Lenore placed a restraining hand on his arm.

"Wait," she said.

Odd waited, and to his shock, the man placed his blade at Lenore's feet.

"I will serve you," he said.

"And me," another put in, driving his sword into the dirt.

"And me."

Around the field it went, until all of them had pledged their blades to Lenore's cause. Odd could only stare at it all as Lenore directed them back toward the miller's home. It shouldn't have been possible for a leader to change men's minds so completely, and yet Lenore had. In that moment, he knew that she was more than any princess.

"You are a queen," he said to her.

Lenore shook her head. "Not yet. But maybe, with Lord Carrick's help, I will be."

CHAPTER THIRTEEN

E rin did her best to train the men who were starting to arrive at the farm. She stood there in front of them with her spear, and she made them stand all in a line while she looked them over, and she did her level best to think of something that would turn these men into a force that would stop Ravin's armies.

In the end, she cut sticks from a nearby tree and set them down in the dirt in front of the men.

"You need to be prepared to fight for each other," she said. "I was there in the fight for Royalsport, and I saw men saved over and over again by the men beside them." She thought of Odd for a moment, and the times that he'd saved her, then of what *else* he'd done. "When one of those people betrays you, *fails* you, it is the worst feeling that there is."

"Why are there sticks here?" one of the men asked. "I have a sword right here."

"A sword you can't use well enough to keep from gutting your partner while you practice," Erin snapped back. It should have been obvious why they were using sticks. More than that, the men should have obeyed instantly. She was a proven fighter, briefly even a Knight of the Spur. She was a princess too. Shouldn't that be enough?

"I can use this sword," the man retorted, hefting it and essaying a couple of swings in the sunlight. To Erin's eye, they looked clumsy and slow. She took up her staff, making sure that the end of it was firmly in place over the blade of the spear.

"Then prove it," she said. "Land one single blow on me, and I'll let you run the training how you want. You don't think sticks are good enough for you? They're good enough for me."

The man started to back away. "That's not what I meant, I—"

"I gave you an order," Erin said, raising her voice. "Hit me, you useless, lily livered—"

She was already ducking as the soldier swung for her, letting her anger at the man's incompetence fuel her as she swung her staff around, taking his legs from under him.

"Worthless," she said. She pointed at another, this one with a sickle in his hand. He was easily the largest man there. "You, help him. Maybe both of you at once can land something. *Do it.*"

They came at her together, and Erin dodged the blow of the sickle, parried a sword stroke, and rammed the butt of her spear into the swordsman's belly. She caught the next sweep of the sickle toward her head, twisted, and sent the weapon flying from the man's hand.

Erin kept going, taking them on in ones and twos, sending them sprawling one after another, and they never even got close to landing anything on her. A part of her wanted to take on all of them at once, wanted to take the cover off her spear's bladed head and show them what *really* happened when they went up against someone like her...

She took a step back, her breath coming short as she tried to get control over her urge to keep fighting, to hurt these men. She looked over them on the ground, some of them wincing with bruises, some of them looking at her in terror as if she might lunge at them and slay them all.

"You're all useless," Erin said. "You're lucky I even think it's worth giving you *sticks*. Now get practicing with them."

She stalked off, heading away far enough that she could start to get her anger under control. She sat on a sack of grain, feeling the fury running through her even now, urging her to lash out.

It wasn't at the men there, of course; it was far larger than that. It was a rage that seemed to include everything within it, from Ravin and his armies for all that they'd done, to Odd, for what he'd *stopped* her from doing, to herself, for all that she'd failed to do...

"I could have saved her," Erin whispered. "I could have."

She sat there for what seemed like a long time. Eventually, Tess came over to her, bringing a plate of lamb and flatbreads.

"I've offered some to the others," Tess said. "But they don't want to stop. It seems like they're scared to."

Erin cursed herself for that. "I went too far with them, but... they can't do this. They're willing enough, but there's a difference between them and real fighters."

"Training," Tess said. "That's the big difference."

"But do we have enough time to train them properly?" Erin asked. It hadn't just been her training with the Knights of the Spur or with Odd that had made her able to fight like this; it had been years of playfighting with Rodry, years of sneaking away to the House of Weapons.

"The sooner you start, the sooner it will be done," Tess said. "And... don't tell them that they can't do it. They need to believe that they can. These men are going to fight for you, maybe die for you. They can't think that it's inevitable that they'll lose." She stepped away. "I'll leave you to think for a moment."

Erin was thinking. She knew that Tess was right, and that she needed to think about the way she was choosing to train these men. She also knew that she needed to do more than that, and she'd known what she needed to do from the moment Lenore and Odd left. It had been part of the reason she stayed behind.

For now, she went back to the men. They were essaying sword cuts at one another with the sticks, parrying and cutting back at one another, occasionally connecting, mostly missing. The men looked round as Erin approached, and she could see the fear there.

She sighed.

"I'm going to show you how to do this better," she said. "You could have beaten me before, when it was two on one; you just need to know how."

She pointed at the first two she'd beaten, drawing them out from the group. She took one of the sticks she'd cut, because she didn't trust herself not to use her spear if she was losing.

She pointed to the big man.

"You have two jobs for this bout," she said. "You block anything that comes at yourself, and anything that comes at him." She pointed at the other man. She turned to the former soldier. "You can strike at me if there's space, but that's your second job. Your first is to protect *him*, understand?"

"Yes," the soldier said.

"Good, then fight."

The first time they tried it, they split up, circling in different directions. Erin struck each of them in turn, declaring them dead. The second time, they got it, sticking together. She lunged at the bigger man, half speed, and the smaller one parried it. She lunged again, and this time the bigger man was in time to catch the blow, while the smaller one managed to sneak his stick through Erin's defenses, tapping her on the shoulder.

"There!" Erin said. "You can do it! Two of you working together just managed to defeat a Knight of the Spur. If you can do that, you can defeat anyone, but you have to work together."

They seemed to get it then, and for the rest of the afternoon, Erin worked them mercilessly, determined that when more troops showed up, each man would be able to show them what she was teaching. She showed them how to fight one beside another, each defending for the next using weapons or makeshift shields, each protecting himself, and each stabbing to his right, at the enemy next to him, striking at the angle no one would think to block.

She showed them how to hit and run next, rushing up to strike a sack of flour as a group and then running back to hiding spots on the farm.

"The goal is not to have a fair fight," she said to the men. "The goal is to win. Strike from ambush. Kill and run away. Strike your enemy from the flank. If you can find bows, shoot them from a distance while they are preparing for a glorious charge. I cannot make you knights, but I can make you into men who can beat the best Ravin has to offer!"

That got a cheer from the men. Erin was just sorry that she was lying to them.

As darkness fell, she let them slip away to their places in the barn or dotted around the farm. Erin went to her own room in the farmhouse, blowing out the candle that lit the room, pretending sleep until the moon was well up and she was sure that everyone else was in their beds.

Then she slipped back downstairs, tiptoeing to the door and releasing the latch that held it closed. She stepped out into the darkness.

It had to be this way, had always been going to be this way from the moment she let her sister and Odd go to Lord Carrick without her. Maybe they would find support, or maybe they wouldn't, but Erin knew the truth: it wouldn't be enough. If the nobles had been enough to defeat Ravin's forces, they would have done it when he invaded. As for the men here … they were good men, brave men, and they would be slaughtered in the first battle.

No, Erin needed to end this her way. Alone, she stood a good chance of being able to get back into Royalsport. Alone, she could slip into the castle unnoticed. She'd always been a good climber, so maybe she could climb the walls. Alone, Erin would have a chance to kill Ravin where an army might not.

She'd heard her sister and Odd talking about why they couldn't just do that, and to Erin's ears, it was nonsense. His army was already causing misery in the kingdom. It was already everywhere. Maybe without a leader, it would be easier to pick off.

The truth was that Erin didn't care. All that mattered to her then was killing Ravin. She'd missed the chance back in the execution of her mother, had missed the chance to *save* her mother. Whatever the political dimensions around it, whatever the aftermath, that meant one thing:

Ravin was hers to kill.

CHAPTER FOURTEEN

Vars wasn't sure if he liked looking like a peasant or not, but at least it meant that he was able to go out of Bethe's home with her, traveling with her as she went to the marketplace, able to keep his head down and keep walking when they passed guards without the risk that they would suddenly recognize him as the king.

Not that it kept the fear out of him. That was ever-present, there with every step, the worries inside him certain that everyone he passed was looking at him, that they all knew who he was, and that there would be assassins coming for him at any moment.

"It's fine," Bethe said beside him. "Everyone has too many of their own concerns to worry about you."

How had she guessed what Vars was so afraid of? He didn't know, but he wanted to snap at her that he was a king, and that she shouldn't speak to him that way. He didn't, of course, and not just because it would only produce another of those slightly amused smiles that seemed to deflect his rage so easily. He couldn't do it here, because there were too many people around.

Vars had thought that he'd known all he needed to about his kingdom. He'd seen poor people before, or at least servants, but now there were whole crowds of them in the marketplace, forming lines before the stalls, waiting for their turn to buy the little that was there under the gaze of the House of Merchants' great façade.

"Why are they waiting so patiently?" Vars asked Bethe. "Why not just push past?"

"Because people need one another," Bethe said. "At a time like this, the ones who start thinking only about themselves are the ones who make things worse for everyone. No one would serve them. No one would help them."

Vars snorted at that, because it didn't fit with anything he'd ever seen when it came to people. People did what they thought they could get away with. Even now, he thought that he could see thieves moving through the crowd, looking for coins, or to snatch things from stalls.

As for the rest, there were men and women there, young and old, all under the watchful gazes of a few guards. There weren't as many of Ravin's soldiers there as there had been, but there were still enough to make Vars's posture hunch more, not wanting to attract attention.

"Why are we even here?" he asked Bethe as they approached the front of one of the lines. "It's not like there's anything here."

As far as he could see, all of the stalls were almost bare, with the produce there so sparse that it seemed like the place had been picked clean by a plague of locusts.

"There's enough for now," Bethe insisted.

Not everyone seemed to think so. One man was complaining loudly to the guards, closer to them than he should have been, large and belligerent. Vars could only stare as the man waved a finger in one of their faces.

"How are we supposed to feed ourselves when your armies take all the food?" he demanded. "And when thieves take from us what they want?"

"Emperor Ravin will provide," one of the guards replied.

The big man spat. "That's what I think of your emperor."

That was the moment when the guards grabbed him, kicking and struggling, dragging him away.

"Another one for the Quiet Men to question," someone said softly, away to Vars's left. Someone else shushed them quickly.

Things were somber as Bethe bought food, and Vars spent the whole time looking around, sure that there would be Quiet Men coming now that someone had spoken against the emperor. When the time came to hurry back to Bethe's small cottage, Vars was only too eager to go.

On the streets around him, he could see the figures who waited in alleys, watching intently, and Vars couldn't work out if they were Quiet

Men or just thieves. He *did* see one home that had been burnt out, people picking through the wreckage for any scrap that they could find.

"Why are they doing that?" Vars asked.

"Because they're desperate," Bethe said. "Everyone is."

She looked around as she said it, as if expecting Quiet Men to jump out at her just for saying it. It was the first time that Vars had seen her react like that, and he wasn't sure that he liked it.

He understood desperation, though, or thought he did. How many times now had he been in positions where he'd done what he needed to do to survive, because there was no other option? He'd only given up the castle because he couldn't think of a better choice, only killed his father because the alternative was his father destroying him.

They made it back to Bethe's house, and Vars was a little shocked to find just how happy he was to be back there. He was used to the luxury of a castle, but now, here in this hovel, he felt ... safe.

"There's a lot going on out there that I hadn't known about," Vars ventured once they were safely back inside.

"It's what happens after wars," Bethe said. "The people suffer, because those better than them decide they want to lay claim to land, and they don't care about the people beneath them. They don't even think about them."

Vars winced at that, because he *certainly* hadn't thought about any of the unwashed poor of the city, except perhaps with mild disgust. Yet now that he knew Bethe, he found himself wondering what things were like for others in the city.

"We need to start baking more bread," Bethe said. That was one thing Vars had learned in his time there: that for most of the people, most of the time, their days consisted of doing the same hard, repetitive things over and over in the hope that it would be enough to get them to the next day, and the next. It was almost enough to make Vars ashamed of the time he'd spent doing almost nothing, yet waking up in silk sheets every day.

Almost, but honestly, it mostly made him long for it again. If he could click his fingers and go back to it all in an instant, he would. Vars could picture it easily, drinking good wine, attending formal balls, having people bow to him with respect, never having to worry about food or shelter or any of the other things that could be taken away here all too easily if people whispered the wrong words to the Quiet Men. He thought of himself there and—

"Vars, you're daydreaming," Bethe said. "We have a lot to do."

Vars nodded, and didn't even offer his usual complaints about being a prince made to work as he started sifting flour and bringing it together. Admittedly, a lot of that was because he knew it wouldn't make any difference to Bethe, but some of it was because he understood just how hard life was for her down in this poor section of the city.

He tried to picture what it would be like if he brought her up into the world of feasts and knights, nobles and courtly manners. She would probably wonder at it all, standing there on Vars's arm while they—

Wait, what was he thinking? He quickly reminded himself of the truth: that he was using this woman for a place to stay and a way to keep clear of Ravin's people. She was a peasant who should mean nothing to a man like him. He was a king, and she was nothing but a baker.

"Knead harder, Vars," Bethe instructed him, awkwardly reminding Vars that *he* was the one who was currently up to his elbows in dough. He did as she told him, and even as he did it, he let his mind wander again, this time to the dissatisfaction of all the people of the city.

Maybe he could do something with it all, he mused. People speaking out individually achieved nothing, and most of the people there didn't have the skills to organize anything more. They were peasants, after all.

Yet what if Vars applied himself to it? He could build support, construct a resistance out of the resentment and the anger within the city. He could create an uprising that would sweep away Ravin faster than his troops had been swept away on the tides the wizard had summoned.

Vars could imagine how it would happen, the people he would have to persuade, or bribe, or kill. He would speak at rallies of the masses, whipping them up into such a frenzy that Ravin's troops would be torn limb from limb by them. He would ride to victory, carried aloft on the arms of those who had supported him. Ravin would be at his mercy, and Vars would make sure that he was never a threat to the kingdom again.

Vars pictured slicing the man's head from his shoulders, while a crowd cheered for him like the hero he was, and Bethe...

Vars stopped himself. She did *not* matter to him like that. She would not. She could not.

As for the rest of it, well, it was a nice thought, but Vars knew better than anyone just how unlikely it was. Ravin was a ruthless and dangerous opponent. To face him would mean Vars risking everything. More than that, it would require the people of the city actually liking him, and Ravin's "King Vars" joke had more than destroyed any chance he had of that. The rumors about him murdering his father probably didn't help with that, either.

So what did that leave, then? If Vars had no real way to retake his throne or gain his revenge, what was left for him? A lifetime of baking bread alongside Bethe and being dismissed with gentle smiles whenever he tried to be too kingly? Maybe a chance to run somewhere when things calmed down.

Vars wasn't sure, and he definitely wasn't going to admit to feeling anything for a mere peasant woman when he'd avoided the attentions of the most determined noblewomen there were, but for now, at least, he was content.

CHAPTER FIFTEEN

Aurelle walked to the castle with an outward appearance of calm, but inside, she was fuming. This was too much for Meredith to ask of her. It was too much to hope to do. To sit there with men she'd sworn to kill and to pretend to be their friend was too much.

Yet if the House of Sighs wasn't that, what was it? Aurelle knew as well as anyone that the men and women there could smile and convince people that they were special, even as they disliked them.

Smiling to men you'd sworn to kill was harder, though.

She walked up to the front gate, because sometimes the best way in was the obvious one. The guards there eyed her openly, and Aurelle wondered if she would have to kill any of them before this was over.

"What are you doing here, woman?" one asked. "Here to offer yourself to the emperor?"

"I'm here to see Duke Viris and his son," Aurelle replied. She managed to make her voice innocent and non-threatening, as if she didn't even understand the suggestion the guard had just made. "My name is Aurelle."

The guards stared at her, then one beckoned over a passing servant, who looked as though she was already far too harassed with all the tasks she had to do.

"You, go to Duke Viris. Tell him that there's a woman here to see him by the name of Aurelle. See if he wants to see her, or if we should throw her into a dungeon to await his attention."

Aurelle suppressed—with difficulty—the urge to lunge forward and cut the guard's throat for that. She stood not showing any of the fear she felt in that moment, because there was always risk in something like this.

Pretending to be someone she wasn't, putting herself at the heart of her enemies, was always dangerous, and times like this were only reminders of that.

Because they *could* kill her. She would probably be able to kill one of these guards easily enough in a straightforward fight, maybe even both if she was lucky, but in truth, even her most violent skills were about killing from the shadows, not openly. After she'd killed them, what then? There was a whole castle full of guards, enough to bring her down easily.

Her best defense in moments like this was not being discovered, sinking into the role she was playing until she *was* who she was pretending to be. That the person in question was herself this time seemed to make it harder, not easier. She had to be a version of herself now that didn't want to kill her former employers, that was still loyal to their cause.

The waiting seemed to take forever, and for every moment of it, Aurelle could practically feel the guards' eyes roving over her. She could tell that they were hoping she was lying, so that they would have an excuse to seize her. She wasn't, but even so, her position felt precarious. What if Duke Viris decided that this was a good moment to be rid of her? What if he simply decided to ignore any connection with her?

Then she would run, come back, and kill him in spite of what Meredith wanted.

Now, Aurelle found herself almost wishing that the duke would try to betray her. She was still picturing all the things that she might do when the servant came back, hurrying as if she'd been told to run.

"The duke and his son say that they will see you immediately, my lady," the servant said. "If you will follow me?"

Aurelle took a step to follow her, and the guard blocked the way. "We still need to search you. For weapons."

"Do you *really* think Duke Viris will appreciate hearing why you delayed me?" Aurelle countered, letting a little of the anger she felt flow into her voice. It was enough that the guard stepped back, letting her pass.

She followed the servant through the castle, seeing more guards, more servants. The interior had changed, the pictures replaced with ones glorifying Ravin, or with scenes from the history of the Southern Kingdom.

There were maps of sections of it now, from the deserts to the grasslands and the cities. There were statues of warriors. There were nobles and officials in the red and purple of Ravin's colors. Some of those nobles were new, southerners Aurelle didn't know. Others were men and women she had met before, and who knew her as Aurelle Hardacre the minor noble.

The servant led her to a suite of rooms as opulent as any there. They were in the middle of redecoration, the drapes and tapestries being changed to the red and purple of the rest of the castle, while a painting of Duke Viris alongside Emperor Ravin was being set in one corner.

Duke Viris and his son sat waiting at a table. Seeing them together, Aurelle could see the similarities between them, in the same elegant sharpness of the features, the same slenderness, and the same hard edge to their gaze.

Aurelle curtseyed, bowing her head mostly because it made it easier to keep the hatred off her face. It would be so easy to lunge forward, to just draw a knife or a strangling wire from within her clothing, and to finish this.

"Aurelle," Duke Viris said. "This is a surprise. When things took so long, I didn't know if you would be back."

"It took time to find the right moment in the midst of the chaos," Aurelle said. "And then it took time to get back from Astare."

"Astare?" Duke Viris said. He must have caught Aurelle's glance over toward Finnal. "Anything you can say to me, you can say in front of my son. He knows all my business, and helped plan this."

That confirmed to Aurelle that Finnal needed to die just as much as his father, right at the moment when she could least afford to do it.

"I initially tried to be subtle, and guide him away from what he might find. Once Prince Greave reached Astare, it was clear that wasn't going to happen."

"And so?" Finnal asked. He leaned forward slightly, almost eagerly.

"It's done," Aurelle said. "The prince is dead."

"How?" Duke Viris asked. Of course he would want to know the details. He gave the appearance of such a cold, calculating man, but Aurelle knew exactly how much he enjoyed all this. As for his son, she'd seen him there in the House of Sighs often enough.

"In the chaos of the initial attack," Aurelle said, but one look at the duke told her that wasn't going to be enough. She had to lie, even if lying about this felt like a fresh betrayal of her beautiful, dead prince. "I let him think that he was leading me to safety. I let him put me on a boat. Then I stabbed him and dropped his body in the bay. No one will find it."

"Good," Duke Viris said. "You and your House have done well, Aurelle."

"I have been told to tell you that I remain at your disposal, Duke Viris," Aurelle said. She bowed her head. "For whatever other tasks you require."

"There is little to do," Duke Viris said. "None of them are left. Princess Lenore and her sister are dead, Vars is gone and can never hope to lead men. Prince Rodry is dead, as are his parents. Now, Prince Greave is gone as well."

"You've cleared the way for a new emperor quite well," Aurelle said. That got a sour look from both the duke and his son.

"We have positioned ourselves as Emperor Ravin's most loyal northern nobles," Finnal said.

"So you're in the same position you were before under King Godwin?" Aurelle said, making it seem like an innocent question, rather than something with barbs.

"The old kingdom was never going to last," Finnal said. He sounded a little disappointed, though.

"So it wasn't the plan for *you* to rule?" Aurelle said, feigning innocent puzzlement.

"Plans change," Duke Viris replied. He drew over a sheaf of paper, making a mark on it, obviously addressing some small piece of business to do with his lands. "For now, at least, we have achieved the best position it is possible to achieve in the circumstances that we have."

"Of course, great men manage to change circumstances," Aurelle said. She smiled at Duke Viris in a way that she hated. "And you *are* a great man, my lord."

"Are you trying to flatter me to keep your position?" Duke Viris said.

76

"Yes," Aurelle admitted, because sometimes letting someone catch you out could be a weapon. It made them think that they were cleverer than you, and that they could catch you out again at will.

Of course, she had to remember that Duke Viris *was* clever, and was dangerous. So was his son.

"As it happens, I will continue to have a need for someone prepared to listen on my behalf. A powerful man will have enemies."

"Especially when they realize that you have made yourself Ravin's heir in all but name," Aurelle said.

"Do not say such things," Duke Viris said, sharply, and Aurelle schooled her features to something apologetic.

"Forgive me, my lord. I merely meant that the emperor has no obvious heir, and that, as the man closest to him in the Northern Kingdom, and as the man who can command the support of the whole kingdom, if something were to happen to him..."

"And if a Quiet Man were to hear you say that," Finnal said, "it would be a slow death, not just for you, but for us as well. We should kill you just for suggesting it."

"And *will* you, my lords?" Aurelle asked. She half hoped that they would say yes, because then she would have an excuse to kill them both and run.

Duke Viris shook his head. "No, you are far too valuable for that. As you say, a man in my position will need help. You will have a place with me, and tasks that will suit your... abilities."

"Thank you, my lord. I am grateful," Aurelle said. She was happy about more than just the position, though. She was happy about the thoughtful look on the duke's face. It was a look that promised a lot, and that, in time, might prove more dangerous than any knife.

Chapter Sixteen

L enore stared up at Lord Carrick's castle home, hoping as she did so that she knew what she was doing. Back at the farm, it had seemed obvious that she should go to get the help of the local lord, but now, with his castle looming over her, it was a reminder of just how big the disparity in their positions was. She had almost nothing at the moment, while he had all of this.

The castle itself was a squat, broad thing, built around an open bailey and with towers set around its walls. Men patrolled those walls, looking out over the surrounding countryside.

"If I remember Lord Carrick," Odd said, "he likes to think of himself as a practical man. He is not a man to be swayed by an impassioned appeal."

The former monk and knight stood beside her, looking up at the defenses as if trying to calculate all the weaknesses in them. Lenore found herself wondering how many he saw.

"What *will* work with him?" Lenore said.

"He cares about what other people think," Odd said. "He strikes out at any who slight him, because he thinks he cannot afford to let anything go. If we can get in to see him, and remind him of his obligations, that might work."

If they could get in to see him. That was the first problem. If Lenore was to persuade Lord Carrick, then it sounded as though she would need to stand in front of him with people around. If she walked up as she was, he might insist on a private meeting, or he might just turn her away, not believing who she was. Maybe he would even turn her away if he *did* know who she was.

Lenore could think of another way to do it though. She turned to Odd. "Come with me."

She led the way to the castle's gate, looking from one guard to another. "We've been sent from Royalsport with urgent messages. We need to speak to Lord Carrick. Is he holding audience?"

Lenore managed to get the right level of urgency into her voice, because the guards didn't question it, just parted, pointing to the keep that sat at the heart of the castle.

"He will be in his hall," one of the men said. He was an older man with a bushy beard that stuck out underneath his guard's helmet. "I will show you the way."

He led the way through an open courtyard, ringed by outbuildings. People there were bustling about their tasks, and everything seemed orderly in a way that it hadn't been anywhere else on their journey. It seemed that everyone had their tasks to perform, and were just getting on with them.

Lenore followed the guard into the keep, going through into a large hall that looked to Lenore far too much like her father's had. Lord Carrick's banners flew on the walls, surrounded by weapons, while trestle tables sat there for his men to eat. The lord himself sat at a table up above, looking out over the rest as he ate.

The man was perhaps her father's age, gray-haired and solidly built, dressed in dark clothes whose slit sleeves showed flashes of white cloth beneath. Gold chains sat around his neck, and he looked out with piercing blue eyes as Lenore approached with Odd.

"My lord," the guard said. "This is—"

"Princess Lenore, daughter of Godwin the Third," Lord Carrick said, placing his hands on the table and standing.

Lenore froze, unsure how to react at being caught out like that, especially when Lord Carrick didn't sound happy about her presence. Lenore glanced across to Odd, reminding herself that she wasn't alone for this. She had his support, at least.

Lord Carrick kept going. "And *that* is Sir Oderick the Mad, knight and murderer. I'd thought you were dead, Sir Knight. I'd *hoped* you were dead."

"There have been days when I hoped it too," Odd said. Lenore could see him looking around at the hall filled with warriors, as if trying to work out which of them might strike first.

"How did you know me so easily?" Lenore asked.

"I have been at court before," Lord Carrick said. "Enough to see you; enough to know who you are. A pretty little princess who did as her mother commanded, if I remember rightly."

He didn't sound impressed, and Lenore knew that with a man like this it wouldn't be enough to be courteous and kind.

"If you know who I am," Lenore said, "shouldn't you be bowing, my lord? My parents are dead, my older siblings are gone, so what does that make *me*?"

He stared at her for a moment or two. "If all of that is true, then there is a case to be made for you being queen."

"Exactly," Lenore said. "And that is a claim that I intend to make real, with the aid of my father's trusted nobles."

"You're talking about going to war," Lord Carrick said. He sat back down and swept an arm toward his men. "You're talking about me giving up my men to you, and risking my position, my life, for your cause."

"For your cause too," Lenore said. She looked around at the men there, then back at Lord Carrick. "You got your position because you served alongside my father, Lord Carrick. You fought by his side. You hold your lands because my father trusted you, and your men follow you because of who you are. You are from a noble family, and without my father, you would still have something, but you would not have all this."

She knew that she had to make that connection. She had to make him see that everything good in his life had come from his association with her family. She had to appeal to his sense of honor, and to his existing ties. He might not help her because it was the right thing to do, but would because it was the orderly, honorable thing to do.

"You recognized me because you were in an honored place at my father's court," Lenore said. "Well, why not have a place like that at *my* court? You fought by my father's side, so why not fight by *my* side? What place will you have in King Ravin's kingdom?"

"You make an interesting point," Lord Carrick said. "Come, sit by me and eat, and we will discuss things further."

To Lenore, it seemed like an important first step. She went up to the top table in the hall, and men and women shuffled to the side, making way for her to sit. Odd didn't sit, but stood at her back, every inch the bodyguard.

"Will you not eat with me, Sir Knight?" Lord Carrick said.

"Odd takes my safety very seriously," Lenore said.

"Odd? Is *that* what he calls himself these days?" Lord Carrick laughed as he looked over to the former knight. "It suits you."

"So my abbot told me."

Carrick laughed again. "The monk's robes aren't a joke? Well then, are you still deadly with a sword? Does your princess have at least that going for her?"

Lenore cut in, because she wasn't about to be ignored by this man. "Odd is quite deadly, yes. Fight beside me, and you will probably get to see it."

"You're determined to push me on that, aren't you?" Lord Carrick said. "Won't you at least eat with me, Princess?"

Lenore took a delicate bite from a goose leg. Then she set that leg back on her plate pointedly. "Lord Carrick, you're trying to deflect me. Would you have done that if it were my father sitting here?"

"Ah, that's the difficulty, you see," Lord Carrick said. "You are a lovely young woman, and from what I remember of my times in Royalsport, you are well versed in the niceties of court, but you are *not* your father."

"I am his oldest remaining heir," Lenore pointed out. "I have the best claim to the throne. If anyone is going to fight back against Ravin's rule, I am the best choice for them to rally around."

"But you are a woman, not a trained war leader," Lord Carrick said. He took a sip of wine.

"I am willing to be advised on such matters," Lenore said. "I have Odd to help me, and my sister Erin rode with the Knights of the Spur. Their efforts helped to slow the invasion of Royalsport."

"And yet, ultimately, they lost," Lord Carrick said.

Lenore's patience was starting to wear thin. "You are finding excuses, Lord Carrick. You are delaying and deflecting, without getting to the heart of this. Once upon a time, you would have come running the moment a ruler raised their banners, calling for help. Now, it seems that you are doing everything you can to avoid giving me a clear answer."

"Because I have not decided what my answer will be yet," Lord Carrick said simply. "You ask me to join your armies, but I have no evidence that you even *have* an army. You are asking me to come out in support of you, against the most ruthless of enemies, risking my life and that of my men. I served with your father, and I fought against uprisings. I have seen how easily they fall, and what can happen to those who engage in them." He gave Odd a pointed look. "Why should I join you?"

"What assurances are you asking for?" Lenore asked. "If it's about the number of other lords who have joined—"

"I'm asking what's in it for me," Lord Carrick said. "Can you offer me increased lands? Gold? Your father was always against the strict enforcement of laws of serfdom, but if you tell me that I will be able to treat peasants as they *should* be treated, we might have a deal."

Lenore thought, trying to work out what to say. She knew that she needed this man's forces, but she also knew that she couldn't betray ordinary people like Harris and Tess in order to do it. She wouldn't become like Ravin in order to beat him.

So she shook her head. "No," she said. "I cannot offer you any of that. I can promise that the world will go back to what it was, and that we will not be ruled over by an emperor who butchers those who oppose him. I can promise you that your existing lands will be safe, and that there will not be Quiet Men stalking your halls. Beyond that, I can't promise anything."

"Ah," Lord Carrick said, standing and stepping back. "Then I think we have a problem. On the whole, I think that Emperor Ravin will give me *far* more if I simply hand you both over to him."

CHAPTER SEVENTEEN

Odd drew his sword in one smooth movement, stepping up to Lenore's side and trying to cover all the angles that men might come at them from. It was impossible to cover them all at once. Fear filled him, not for himself, but for Lenore.

"Stay behind me," he told her, as he hauled at the edge of the trestle table, flipping it onto its side. At least this way he had a barricade, something to slow down the flood of men who lay beyond.

Those spread out in a rough circle, and Odd tried to calculate which of them might come at him first to try to get to the princess. Who looked confident, and who looked afraid? Who was going to charge in to try to grab the glory of being the one to cut down Oderick the Mad, and capture Lenore? Who was going to risk being first when they had to know that the first man would die?

"What are you waiting for?" Lord Carrick demanded. "Take them! I want the princess alive, but you can kill the knight."

Odd lunged in that moment, smashing aside a man and grabbing Lord Carrick. His lordship might have fought beside King Godwin, but now he was out of practice, and Odd fought off his attempt to break free. He twisted Lord Carrick's arm behind his back, hard enough that he got a yelp of pain from the other man.

He put his sword to the lord's throat. "Tell your men to put down their weapons."

"How about you put *yours* down, and I let you live?" Lord Carrick countered. "I told them to kill you, but I could just as easily let you walk away. Go back to wherever you disappeared to the first time, Sir Oderick. Go back into obscurity. We only care about the princess. Emperor Ravin probably won't even kill her. He'll probably just keep her in a dungeon somewhere, or ship her back to the Southern Kingdom."

Odd snarled, and for once the old anger threatened to break through. He wanted to cut this man down, wanted to charge into all of them and kill them one after another, but he knew it wouldn't work. Instead, he forced Lord Carrick forward, using the grip on his arm to guide him.

"Stay close to me," he said to Lenore, and she fell into place behind them, the form of Lord Carrick serving as a shield for both of them.

"Archers!" Lord Carrick ordered, and already there were men snatching bows down off the walls. More came in with the weapons.

"You think I won't cut your throat if they fire?" Odd demanded, even as a ring of arrows began to surround the three of them.

"Perhaps," Lord Carrick said. His hand crept up toward Odd's sword. Odd wrenched at his other hand to stop it, but it made no difference. Now Lord Carrick had a hand between the blade and his throat. "Or perhaps I will hold this here long enough to let my archers bring you both down. The princess's body will not be as good as her living, but it will be something."

"Then it seems we're stuck," Odd said.

"I have a proposal," Lord Carrick said. "A contest of champions. My man against you. If I win, the princess is mine to give to the Emperor. If you win, you get to go free."

"No." To Odd's surprise, that came from behind him, from Lenore.

Odd glanced back to her. "I can do this."

"No," she said. "You will not."

"Lenore—"

"Queen Lenore," she reminded him. Gently, but it was still a rebuke. "And I did not come here to slink out, holding a hostage, Odd. Nor did I come here to be fought over as if I am merely a prize to be won."

"It's the only way I can get you out of here," Odd said, but Lenore stepped past him.

"I know you want to protect me," she said. "But this is not the way. I came here to get Lord Carrick's men for my cause, and I mean to have them. Now, release Lord Carrick."

"My queen—" Odd began, but Lenore gave him no chance to complete his objection.

"Now, Odd," she commanded.

Odd did it, tossing Lord Carrick away from him, so that the lord went stumbling.

"Kill the monk," he commanded, even as he climbed up to his knees.

A man rushed forward, and Odd stepped to meet him, his blade sweeping out toward the man's throat. It took his head from his body, and in the pause that followed, Odd could see plenty of others getting ready to attack. Too many, even for him to fight.

"Wait!" Lenore ordered, and to Odd's surprise, many of the men *did* wait. "I came here today for your help. I asked your lord for it, and he refused, then tried to betray me. Now I'm asking you directly."

Odd saw her sweep an arm around toward Lord Carrick.

"You know what kind of man your lord is," she said. "The kind of man who mistreats those around him, who does whatever is most profitable for him. The kind of man who would sell his own rightful queen to an enemy if there was a profit in it. The kind who would sacrifice any of *you* in a heartbeat."

To Odd, it seemed as if the room was holding its breath. He had seen Lenore do this with farmers and with bandits, but these men were neither. They were hardened warriors, who had obviously killed for their lord many times before.

"He was going to sacrifice one of you just a minute ago," Lenore said. "A single combat? Which of you truly believes that you could have lived against Sir Oderick the Mad? Or maybe that wasn't the plan. Maybe he was just giving his word so that he could get clear of Odd's sword, and then he would order us butchered. It is the kind of man he is."

Odd saw Lord Carrick's flicker of annoyance at that.

"What are you waiting for?" he demanded, shoving a couple of his men in front of him. "Attack!"

"You *could* attack," Lenore said. "But notice the way he's sneaking back behind you. That's because he knows the truth: the first to do it will die, and the second, and probably the third. You know how deadly Odd is. You've heard the stories. You could do that, or you could ask yourselves what sort of men *you* are."

Looking around, Odd could see the thoughtful looks on the faces of many of the men there.

"You could ask yourself what's worth fighting, and maybe dying, for," Lenore said. "Is it worth fighting to hand one woman to a man you know will kill her, but probably only after he's taken the time to torture her? Or is it worth fighting for your home, to protect it from an invasion that will not touch a man like Lord Carrick, but that will take everything from the people you know?"

"Enough of this!" Lord Carrick roared. "Kill Sir Oderick, take the girl. Do it now!"

Inevitably, some men came forward. Odd leapt to meet the first, striking him down with a single blow. He turned to smash aside a cut aimed at his head, then shoulder barged a man who was reaching for Lenore. A man came at him, and Odd brushed aside the next blow, moved inside, and smashed his forehead into the man's face.

More came, and he and Lenore gave ground together, back toward the table, and the one spot in the room he had even a sliver of a chance of defending. A sword came for Odd's head, and he blocked rather than ducking because he didn't want to risk the blow striking Lenore. The impact jarred his hands, almost sending the sword from his grip. Another blow came in from the side, and Odd twisted aside from it, but not quite enough. It scraped along his ribs, bringing sudden pain even as he struck back to take a man's head from his shoulder.

Agony shot through his thigh, and Odd looked down to see an arrow sticking from it. He parried another sword stroke even as his leg gave way, thrusting up from ground level to take another foe in the stomach while the impact of his body with the floor rang through him.

Then there were men standing over him, swords raised, ready to strike. Odd struggled to raise his sword to fight back, but he knew it was hopeless like this. The most he could do was try to take another of them with him, and even then, it would do nothing to save Lenore. He'd failed her. All his efforts, and he hadn't even been able to save her when it mattered.

He saw one of the swords start to descend toward him, and Odd braced himself for the pain, but then there was another sword intercepting it.

"For the queen!"

Odd looked around in astonishment as those of Lord Carrick's men Lenore had managed to convince took on those she had not. Men slammed into those who fought for Lord Carrick. They struck out with swords, and grabbed at arms to hold back those who were still intent on fighting.

Coming at them from the side like that, their numbers swept over their fellows, swords finding a home in flesh some of the time, but more often, men just grabbing Odd's would-be killers and wrenching swords from their hands. Lord Carrick's obedient men fought back, and quickly the sound of clashing swords filled the air.

Even as the two factions within the hall fought, Odd saw one of Lord Carrick's men heading for Lenore, an axe raised to end things. Odd reacted on instinct, throwing himself forward even though he couldn't get to his feet, hacking out at calf level to cut the man's legs from under him. The axe clattered to the floor as the man went down, and Odd cut out from where he lay again, finding the man's throat this time.

Around Odd, the fight continued, but the men who had responded to Lenore's call had the advantage of surprise. In just seconds, it was done. All of Lord Carrick's loyal men were down or disarmed, and Lenore leaned over to help Odd back to his feet. He took the help gratefully, leaning on her because he was sure that his leg would give way if he did not.

Lenore pointed to Lord Carrick.

"Put him in the dungeon of this castle," she said. "The rest of you, decide if you want to fight for me or not. Those who will not may leave and return home, but with no weapons to fight against my cause. Those of you who will serve me, get ready to march."

"I might have trouble marching," Odd whispered to her, eying the arrow still sticking from his body. He knew it would have to come out, and dreaded the damage it might do on the way.

"We'll find you a horse," Lenore promised him.

"You did it," Odd said. "You actually did it."

Lenore looked at him, then at the men. "It's a start, but we still have a lot to do. I will retake my kingdom, Odd."

"And I will be by your side as you do it," he promised.

CHAPTER EIGHTEEN

M aster Grey crouched by the side of the road, the white of his robes billowing around him as he built a construction out of sticks, twine, and feathers. With each piece he placed, he put in a breath of magic.

The object he made was no bigger than his hand, yet it took all of his concentration to do it. The working of power was a delicate thing, especially when trying to locate something as potentially dangerous as the amulet that had been lost. Linking to it too overtly might be as bad as touching it, and Master Grey felt more than old enough, without the amulet's enervation added to it.

When it was done, a leaf sat at the heart of a living cage, turning freely. He felt the moment when the spell connected to the amulet, saw the leaf twist urgently, and Master Grey was shocked to find it pointing back to the place he'd left in search of it, back toward Royalsport, back toward home.

A thrill of fear ran through Master Grey then, and he hoped to any gods that were listening that the amulet had not ended up in Ravin's hands. A man like that would use the power for his own ends, and the suffering would be immense.

Still, there was no reason yet to believe that it was in the newly crowned emperor's hands. Not that *that* necessarily meant things were any better. There were too many others who would cause untold damage with an object like that.

He was being too dramatic, though, he decided as the leaf crumbled to dust in its cage. Most of those who touched the amulet would simply die. Probably even the emperor. As ways of gaining comfort went, that one seemed a little hollow.

Master Grey set off back toward Royalsport, and as he did so, his robes shifted in color, becoming the dull brown of a traveling tinker's. He stepped out onto the road just as a cart came past.

"Hoy there, old man!" the burly man driving it said as he reined in his horses. He had a boy with him who had the same square features, the same set of the shoulders. Obviously his son. "What are you doing out on the road here?"

"I'm on my way to Royalsport," Grey answered.

"Then you'd best climb on my cart," the man said. "It's not safe to be walking out these ways alone."

A part of Grey wanted to point out that he'd walked far more dangerous ways in the past, ways that would have driven lesser men mad. He would be walking those ways now except that he needed his strength for what was to come, and because he needed to be sure that he could make use of his tracking device safely.

For now, it made sense to sit on the back of a cart filled with fish from the coast, waiting while the carter flicked the reins to set his ponies pulling it again.

"I'm Eavis," the man said. "This is my boy, Ned."

The boy gave Grey a shy wave.

"Llywid," Grey said, giving his name in a very old tongue because honest men deserved better than outright lies, but also did not deserve the danger of the truth.

"A strange name," Eavis said. "You aren't a southerner, are you?"

Grey laughed at that. "I've been called many things in my days, but not that. You're going to Royalsport for market?"

"They say there's not enough food there right now," Eavis said. "Prices might be high for once."

Grey thought it more likely that Ravin's men would seize the contents of the cart, and probably take the boy for the army, because even if he was young, he was still old enough to die for the emperor. He thought about that a little as it rumbled on.

"Why are *you* going to Royalsport?" the boy asked, and if his father had been too courteous to ask the question of a stranger in need, he was certainly listening to the answer now.

"Oh, I'm off in search of a magical amulet," Grey said, with a grin that made it seem like a lie even when it wasn't. "One that can suck the life right out of someone if they aren't careful."

The boy gave a small gasp, and his father smiled. "So you're a storyteller then?"

"Sometimes," Grey agreed. "I tell people things they need to hear."

"Royalsport seems like a dangerous place to go to ply your trade," Eavis said. The cart rumbled on beneath Grey.

"It wasn't the direction I was expecting to go, certainly," Grey said. "But needs must."

It was surprisingly good company as their cart rolled its way toward Royalsport. The boy demanded stories, and so Grey told him tales of the kings who had come after the fall of the dragons, of the wars that had been before in the Northern Kingdom. It passed the time, but it also reminded Grey of the reasons why he was doing all that he did.

Eventually, Royalsport came into view, and they stopped briefly, eating hard bread and cheese by the side of the road. Eavis was kind enough to share his, and that had Grey thinking about a different kind of story. He'd heard it himself as a boy, of the man who helped a tinker only to find out that he was a king, or a spirit in disguise, or something else that would grant a boon when revealed.

Grey had only one boon to give this pair. He started to concentrate, focusing in on the left rear wheel of the cart. He thought about the wood there, and the iron pin holding it in place. He thought about the ways wood might rot and weaken, one small fragment leading to the next. This wasn't like water, because wood did not flow and change in the same way, but it was at least something that had the memory of being living. All Grey had to do was remind it of that life, so that it expanded, and shifted, and split …

There was a crash as the rear of the wagon fell to the ground, fish spilling from it.

"Damn it!" Eavis said. "The wheel's gone. It will take most of a day to get that right, and even then, by the time it's done, the fish will be rotten. We might as well go home."

"That's bad luck," Grey said, although it was probably better luck than the alternatives.

"Bad luck for you too," Eavis said. "Looks like you're walking from here, my friend."

"I'll manage," Grey said. He set off, and if he tucked two thick gold coins in behind the wheel as he left, maybe that was just him growing soft in his old age.

He walked the rest of the way to Royalsport, pausing a couple more times along the way to put a fresh leaf into the cage of sticks he had built. Each time, the leaf withered and decayed, but not before it had pointed decisively at the city. Grey sighed and kept walking. He'd been hoping it would be easier than that. As he walked, his robes shifted again, to something darker still.

When he reached the gates, there were plenty of people waiting, and Grey waited among them until he reached the guards. One put a hand on his chest, and it took all of Grey's self-control not to react.

"Hold there, old father, where do you think you're going?"

"I have business in the city," Grey said.

"Begging business by the look of it," the guard said.

Again, Grey had to hold himself back. "I'm no beggar," he said. "I am a scholar, and have been sent to arrange contracts at the House of Merchants, since it is assumed that the legal arrangements have changed under our new emperor."

"If you're really a scholar here for what you say," the guardsman said, "you will know the tax on contracts in the south."

Grey hesitated a moment, and he could see the guard ready to pounce, but Grey smiled then. Did they honestly think that there was a book in the House of Scholars he hadn't read?

"Three percent at the time of signing," Grey said, "in addition to all other taxes."

"And the penalty for drunkenness within a hundred paces of Emperor Ravin's tower?"

"That is a trick question," Grey said, "because the penalty for *anyone* that close to the emperor's tower without permission, drunk or not, is death."

Even so, the guard frowned.

"A scholar would come on a horse," the guard said. "A scholar would have coin."

"I have coin," Master Grey said. "My superiors suggested that there would be a ... gate fee for entry to the city. I believe that in many of the cities of the south it is set at a single quarter shilling."

One good thing about all of this was that Grey was getting to do things he hadn't done in years. When had he last had to bribe a guardsman? Grey took out the coin, holding it in front of the guardsman. Grey wondered if he'd judged this right as the man hesitated; after all, it had been a long time.

Then he snatched it up and nodded, stepping aside to let Grey past.

"All right," he said. "Go about your business."

Grey intended to do exactly that. He hurried into the city, and he *did* head to the merchant district first, if only because it offered such good access to the rest of the city. Around him, he saw people fighting over the goods on stalls, saw a man being dragged away by the guards when he complained about them taking his stock. Eavis would never know the favor Grey had done him.

Grey could pick out the eyes of the Quiet Men upon those in the crowd, but once he knew where they were looking, he also knew where they were not looking, and it was an easy enough thing to find an alleyway where he could take out his tracking device once more. Finding a leaf was harder, and in the end he had to go back into the market, filching a scrap from the edge of a cabbage while no one was looking. He hadn't done *that* in a long time, either.

With his device working again, he looked out over the city, trying to take in the direction the leaf was pointing before it withered. He frowned as he saw it pointing directly, unequivocally, at the painted exterior of the House of Sighs.

"There?" he said aloud. "Why by all the gods would it be hidden *there*?"

CHAPTER NINETEEN

Vars still couldn't believe how well he and Bethe were getting along. He had nothing in common with this peasant woman, had lived a life about as far removed from hers as it was possible to get, and yet he felt more comfortable around her than he had around any of the women of the court.

Perhaps it was because there were no games with her. Bethe said what she thought, and wasn't afraid to tell Vars when he was doing things wrong. *No one* did that. Currently, she was in the front room of the hovel, telling him that he was folding the laundry wrong.

"No, you need to fold it gently, without pressure, or it will crease," she said.

Vars did as she suggested, and she seemed pleased by it. For some inexplicable reason, that made him happy. Once again, Vars had to remind himself that he was just using her to stay safe.

Still, as long as he was here, he might as well at least try to be friendly.

"What was your husband like?" Vars asked. "Did he help you to do all this?"

Bethe shook her head. "He used to go out to work, because people always needed a woodworker. He would help when there was building to be done, and occasionally he would make small trinkets to sell at the market."

Vars could see how sad just talking about it made Bethe, and for some reason, he found that it mattered to him that she was upset.

"I'm sorry," he said, and he didn't know whether he was apologizing for what had happened to her husband, for bringing up the subject, or just for not being him.

"It's all right," Bethe said. "It's just—"

They were interrupted by the sound of a fist hammering on the door.

"Guards! Open up!"

Vars and Bethe stared at one another for a moment. Vars could feel the terror building in his chest, so that it felt like he couldn't breathe. It was only when Bethe pointed at the door to the back room that Vars knew he should be moving.

"I'm coming," Bethe said. "Let me put this washing down."

Vars was already running for the back room, hiding there behind the door, knowing in his heart that it wouldn't be enough. They'd found him! Somehow, the searching guards had found him. He should never have gone out of the house to market with Bethe. He should never have *stayed* here when he should have been running, not until he was far across the sea and no one could find him. He stood there, pressed against the door, leaving it open just a crack so that he could see out into the room beyond.

Bethe opened the door, letting in two of Ravin's soldiers, wearing red tunics and gilt-edged plates of armor. They looked a little different from the guards Vars had seen around the city, cleaner and with more ornamental scrolling on the hilts of their swords. Vars guessed that they had come from the castle itself. Had Ravin sent his best men to seize him?

"You are the woman, Bethe?" one of them said. He was powerfully built, with whorls tattooed on his arms that suggested to Vars that he'd come from one of the desert tribes of the Southern Kingdom's wastes.

"Of course she is," the other said. "Look at her." This one was a little taller than the other, with shaven dark hair and a triangular beard.

Vars kept perfectly still, not daring to even finish closing the door. His fear pinned him in place, unable to do more than watch, and listen, and wait.

"You are to be honored, woman," the first guardsman said. "Emperor Ravin takes the finest women of his kingdom to his bed, and those who please him are rewarded. His officials have heard of your beauty, and now it is clear that this is true. You will come with us."

Emotions rushed through Vars, tangling with one another as they burst inside him. Relief came first, of course, because these men weren't here to find him, to capture him, to kill him. He was surprised to find anger rising alongside it though, at the thought that these men could just come and take Bethe from here, from *him*.

What was he thinking? It was good that they'd come for her, because it meant that they weren't there to find him.

"What?" Bethe said. "No!"

"You would refuse your emperor?" the taller one demanded. "In the south, the noblest families fight with one another to present their most beautiful daughters and wives."

"No," Bethe repeated. "I'm not some whore for him to snap his fingers and demand."

"You are his subject!" the first guard said. "And a woman in a conquered kingdom! You will come with us, now!"

"No!" Bethe shouted back, starting to edge away from the men.

In the moment that they grabbed for her, Vars *wanted* to leap out, to fall on them and beat them senseless for what they were trying to do. For the first time in his life, he truly wanted to be a hero, wanted to be the kind of man that his brother had been, or his father.

Fear still kept him there though, and Vars cursed himself for that even as the guards grabbed at Bethe.

She didn't seem to be about to stand there and let them drag her away, though. She broke free of the men's grips, and as they grabbed for her again, she swung a punch at the taller one that most warriors would have been proud of. It connected with the side of the guard's face, hard enough that he reeled from it. It didn't fell him though, only made him angry enough that he struck back, and Vars heard the crack of that blow even from where he hid behind the door. He had to bite back a cry of anger at the sight of Bethe being hurt like that.

As Bethe turned toward him, Vars could see that her eye was swollen up now from the force of the blow, the skin beneath split by it.

"Idiot!" the shorter guard shouted. "The emperor won't want her like *this*!"

"Then leave me alone," Bethe snapped at them. "Get out of my house!"

For a moment, Vars felt hope, but it was only for a moment. He knew better than Bethe just how cruel people could be, mostly because he'd been as cruel as any of them before now.

"You might not be good enough for the emperor now," the tall one replied. "But you're still more than pretty enough for us. When we're done, we'll cut your throat and display you out on the street so that all know the price of refusing the emperor anything!"

They grabbed for Bethe and again, and Vars wanted to lunge out from his hiding place to take them on. Again though, fear froze him in place, holding him there even as the guards held onto Bethe's arms, dragging her across the floor of the hovel step by step.

Vars's fears only increased as they brought her directly toward the door he was hiding behind.

"There will be a bed back here somewhere," the tall one said. "Come on, bring her."

Vars panicked in that moment, caught between the urge to help and the far more urgent need to survive. He looked around the room, trying to find a hiding place even as one of the men hit Bethe again. His eyes settled on the wardrobe, and Vars turned for it.

He stumbled as he did it, half tripping, and the door came open, leaving him staring in terror at the two guardsmen trying to drag Bethe there. For a moment, it seemed that everyone was still, everything balanced.

Then it seemed that fear and the need to help were both pulling in the same direction for practically the first time in Vars's life. He flung himself at the guards, partly because he wanted to help Bethe, but mostly because the raw, animal terror of what would happen if he didn't propelled him forward.

For a second, the guards didn't seem to know what was happening. Vars slammed into them, the raw ferocity of it making them take a step back, losing their grip on Bethe as they did so. Vars actually managed to get a punch in against one of them, feeling the impact against the man's face, but mostly feeling the pain of his knuckles bruising.

Then the shorter, stockier one recovered from his shock enough to smash a return punch into Vars's stomach, hard enough that Vars doubled over, retching. The tall one hit him then, sending him sprawling to the floor.

They started kicking him, pain bursting over him as their boots connected with his stomach, his ribs, his back. It was all Vars could do to cover his head with his hands, taking the impacts that might have slammed into his face on his forearms instead.

Vars tried to rise, tried to fight back, tried to do any of the heroic things that might have actually saved his life. It just earned him a punch to the face, and now the guards were standing over him, swords in their hands.

"Someone thought he was going to be a hero," the stocky one said. "Well, bad news. Now you're just going to die."

"Wait..." Vars tried. "I'm..."

His head was swimming too much even to declare who he was to try to save his life. He could only stare as the tall one raised his sword to stab down.

The point of a knife appeared from the front of his throat as Bethe stabbed him from behind with a kitchen knife. He stood there, blinking in incomprehension as he died, and in the moments he took to do that, Bethe was already leaping at the second one from behind, stabbing again and again with her knife.

He toppled as well, and now Vars was lying between the two dying guards, the pain in him too much to even begin to stand. His head was swimming, and he was sure that he felt a loose tooth somewhere in his mouth.

Bethe was there then, helping him to his feet. The look of concern on her face was something Vars had never seen before.

"Thank you," she said. She looked like she might say more, but then shook her head. "Thank you."

Vars wanted to laugh at that, wanted to point out that he had done it out of sheer terror, but he didn't. Part of it was that it still hurt too much to talk, but more of it was because this was the first time he could remember that anyone had genuinely thanked him like this, or looked at him like he was heroic, or seen him as more than a coward.

He was surprised to find that he liked it.

CHAPTER TWENTY

As the dragons passed over the Northern Kingdom, Nerra looked down with a sense of wistful longing. This had been her home once, and there was something about seeing it rolling beneath her that made her think of the past.

The future is what matters, Shadr said. *Our future.*

Nerra nodded, because she could imagine that future, and it was glorious. The world would know dragons again, and serve them as it always should have.

It helped assuage her homesickness that the landscape below wasn't truly the one Nerra had known. They were flying across the high north of the kingdom, far from Royalsport, avoiding all the major towns, while the dragons towing the rafts of the Lesser and the Perfected guiding ships did so on a winding path around the northern coast. Until the moment they struck, they wanted as little news as possible of their arrival to spread.

The dragons helped with that. Those who could breathe mists and smoke did so, making it so that from the ground, they must have been only dim shapes, wreathed in cloud. Being so far north helped too. Up here, it didn't matter if the occasional person saw them. They were too far from anywhere to say anything, and no one would believe it anyway if they *did* tell what they saw.

Nerra looked around at the flocking horde of dragons soaring behind Shadr in a wedge shape, gliding on wings of every hue. Who could possibly believe something like this?

They flew, and their flight ate up the distance to Astare almost languidly, giving the dragon pulled ships time to meet them at their destination. From Shadr, Nerra had the impression of some great, shared communication between the dragons, less precise at such a distance, but still enough to make sure the flotilla would arrive when it should. Nerra clung to Shadr's back throughout, trusting to the dragon queen completely.

They passed over the kingdom completely, striking its east coast and heading south, toward the spot where Astare sat. Now, Nerra could see the flotilla again, dragons straining at the ends of great ropes to pull rafts of the Lesser, ships piloted by the Perfected cutting through the water alongside them. Idly, Nerra thought about Leveros, still further east, wondering if it was worth descending on the monks there, taking the island from them. They had the forces to do it easily, even before thinking of the dragons.

Eventually, Shadr said. *But not yet. They are not the ones with the amulet, after all.*

"I might have guessed wrong," Nerra pointed out. "It might not be in Astare."

I trust you, as you trust me. If it is not in this human place, then we shall descend upon the next. So long as we do it before they can use the amulet, that is all that matters.

Nerra could only agree with that. She'd seen the devastation the amulet could cause, the beauty of dragon-kind ripped from the skies by the evil workings of human things. Nerra had seen so much of that evil in her brief human life, seeing all the things that people did to the world, hunting and ravenous, trying to impose themselves on it even though they could never match the beauty or the wisdom of the dragons.

Nerra was still thinking about that when Astare came into view, the darkness of its stone inner city set against the coast, the contrast obvious between the regular lines of its black slate inner city and its chaotic outer city obvious. That contrast between the ancient and the modern was the first thing she saw.

The second thing was the evidence of fire, down at its docks, and within the inner city. Nerra could see the blackening from it there, and the wreckage of the dock. As they flew closer, she could see people working to rebuild it.

She could also see the army there, sitting outside it, red and purple uniforms easy for her sharpened senses to pick out. Those uniforms were not those of the Northern Kingdom, and Nerra found her mind casting itself back to the lessons she'd learned in her childhood. Shock ran through her, sharp enough that she had to cling tighter to Shadr's back to avoid toppling from it.

"The Southern Kingdom?" she said. "King Ravin has taken Astare."

Those soldiers were gathered in massed ranks outside the city, encamped in blocks around campfires, tents set up to maintain order. More soldiers went through the streets, patrolling or standing over work gangs as they worked to repair the damage in the city.

Once upon a time, the implications of that would have broken her heart, because to get here, how much more must the southerners have taken? What would have happened to the people Nerra knew and cared about, as that attack came? What would have happened to her sisters and her brothers?

She knew that she should have felt crushing grief at it all, should have been terrified of what was happening, should have been so many things. Instead, while those feelings were there somewhere, it seemed as if they were buried deep inside her. Instead, she had other feelings at the sight of so many armed humans, ranging from contempt at the difference between them and dragons to apprehension at what was going to come. One feeling was shared between both parts of her, though: anger.

"Kill them," Nerra said, loud enough that it carried even over the rush of the air around her. "Kill them all."

Yes, Shadr replied, and banked inland, the rest of the dragons following in formation. She wheeled around the city until they were approaching it from the landward side, forming a long line, their wings beating in concert as they let the mist around themselves dissipate to allow those below to see what was coming.

Now. The word echoed in Nerra's head and she saw the dragons respond, their wings tucking as they dove at the massed ranks of King Ravin's soldiers. Now, Nerra could make out the screams from below, could see men rushing to arm themselves while others simply ran. Nerra found herself enjoying that moment, even though she was never normally one to enjoy the pain of others. *These* men deserved it.

She saw Shadr's mouth open wide, and black flames poured out, while around her, flames came from all the dragons who descended on the Southern Kingdom's forces. Tents burst into flames, and people's uniforms, and people. Shadr came in low enough that her claws could snatch up a soldier, and those claws ripped him in half, dropping the carcass down onto the waiting troops below. Shadr's swoop carried them up again, and she whirled round as Nerra clung to her.

Some of the dragons landed among the army, lashing out with claws and teeth and tails. The ones who had risen into the air again swooped once more, breathing lines of fire and lightning, frost and acid. Shadr swooped down on another cluster of soldiers, and now she breathed darkness that killed, so that Nerra saw only bodies as it passed.

Shadr landed this time, and men came at her. Nerra leapt down from her back, and a soldier lunged at her with an arming sword. Nerra wasn't armed, but she didn't need to be. She swayed aside from the blow, and her claws were more than sharp enough to punch through armor, through flesh, through everything. She saw Shadr whip her tail around, sending men flying. A sword scraped along Nerra's side, but her scales were thick enough to stop it from being more than a graze with such a glancing blow. She struck back, opening the soldier's throat, sending blood to burst into the air.

More of the Perfected were on the ground now with her, their dragons fighting beside them, or taking to the air again. She saw Shadr snatch up a man in her jaws, crunching down on flesh and bone, saw another dragon lash out with sword-like claws.

The soldiers tried to strike back. Nerra saw one of the Perfected fall, brought down by a sword thrust through his chest. She saw men jabbing at a great yellow-scaled dragon with spears, and if none of them struck anywhere vital, even so, there were enough to wound it through the gaps in its scales.

Nerra saw a group of men trying to flee into the countryside beyond, and her first instinct was to just let them, but Shadr was already taking to the air again.

None may escape. None can speak of us before we have the amulet!

Several of the dragons went with her, chasing any who fled in the direction of the open ground. More were fleeing in the direction of the city, and those were the ones Nerra went after, snatching up a spear so that she could plunge it into the back of a fleeing foe, knocking aside an axe stroke from a man who turned at bay. Nerra caught the weapon and ripped it from the man's hands, even though he was larger than her, the density of her muscles now far greater than any human thing's.

The outer city was starting to burn now as dragons swept over it, turning the houses to candles and bonfires, destroying them in great booming explosions that sent rubble flying. Nerra and the others pursued the soldiers as they tried for a fighting retreat into the walled part of the town, probably hoping that the ancient black walls could stop the attack where nothing else could.

They were still running when the hordes of the Lesser came in from the side of the city that backed onto the ocean, slamming into the soldiers from the far side, howling and snarling as they poured over them in a tidal wave of blood and death. Nerra barely had to fight now, only watch as men were torn apart and devoured, slain in their dozens, their hundreds.

Nerra felt the pressure of the wing beats as Shadr came in to land beside her. The dragon had blood around her jaws, and her presence created a ring of stillness that no one tried to enter. The one man who came at her was met with a blast of shadow that flung him back into the mass of Lesser.

Around her, men died, and buildings burned. The Lesser gorged on flesh and the Perfected strode among it all, controlling them. Second by second there were fewer human things left, until at last Nerra was alone with Shadr at the heart of it all. Satisfaction burned through Nerra, and pride, even as there was the sense that this was only the beginning.

The city of Astare was theirs.

CHAPTER TWENTY ONE

G reave couldn't pretend to be a great woodsman, but he had read enough on the ways of the wild, and he had listened to his sister Nerra describing how to exist in the forest. Combine that with some sharpness of observation, and determination to find the man he had met on the road, and he was at least able to find some tracks.

They weren't much, a thread caught on a bush here, the imprint of a boot tip in the mud there, a few broken branches, and plants pushed aside as the other man had run.

If Greave found him, he would be able to convince him. He would offer the man money to keep silent, or appeal to his better nature. What was it the philosopher Strennus had written in his *On the Nature of Man*? That men were fundamentally good, but sometimes needed to be convinced of it? That men would do the right thing, if only they could be shown the importance of it?

He pushed aside thoughts of Merrick's *On Rulership,* where he pointed out that men were fundamentally untrustworthy, and that it was almost always easier to kill them than it was to pay them or convince them. He wasn't that man. He couldn't be.

Greave's tracking grew easier once he realized that he knew where he was. They were getting closer to Royalsport, and it seemed that the man he was following was heading for it. Greave tried not to think about all the reasons he might be doing that. The biggest fear was that he was trying to tell someone that he'd seen Greave alive. Greave had to find him and convince him before he reached the city.

By the time he caught up with the other man, darkness was falling. In fact, Greave was fairly sure that he only caught up at all because his quarry thought that he'd lost him, and had decided to make camp before heading to the city. The glow of the man's campfire drew Greave in like a moth from the dark, and he padded forward, trying to remember the quiet way Aurelle had moved. With her, every foot had been planned, every movement deliberate and controlled. Greave did it, stilling even his breathing until he got to the edge of a small clearing, where a campfire sat, and a bedroll. The man who had approached him earlier was there, roasting some indefinable meat over that flame.

Greave stared at him, taking in again his greater size, his toughened appearance. He took a breath, still trying to work out the best way to do this, and trying to force himself to pretend confidence.

"I didn't get your name before," he said, stepping out into the clearing like it was nothing that he'd found this man. "But then, you left in a rush."

"Yan," the man said, the answer obviously coming from sheer shock as he stared at Greave. "What are you doing here, your highness?"

"Following you," Greave said. Without being asked, he sat on the other side of the fire. "We need to talk."

The other man stared at him, obviously caught out by the brashness of Greave's approach. That was why he'd done it that way. If he caught this man off guard, he had a better chance of keeping control of this situation.

"You were heading the other way before," Greave said. Judging by the stars above, he glanced off in the direction Royalsport lay. "Yet now you're heading for the capital. Why?"

"Maybe you've reminded me of my duty to the nation," Yan said. "Maybe I'm heading back to join the fight against the oppressors."

Greave winced at that, because how was he going to persuade a man like this to walk away from the goodness of his heart? Even so, he tried that first.

"I know that you're thinking of telling people about me," he said. "You know that will mean me being hunted. It will make it harder for me to do the things I need to do. You might or might not want to fight against King Ravin and his people, but you can do just as much good simply by walking away."

The big man laughed at that. "And where would the profit be in that? It's not like you're going to achieve anything, and this way, at least I make a little coin out of it all."

That brought Greave to the option that seemed more likely to work. He took out his coin pouch.

"How much do you want? King Ravin might pay you, or might just have you tortured, then killed. *I* can pay you right now. You can have the money and stay safe, start a life somewhere else."

"Or maybe I take your money, then have King Ravin's on top," Yan said.

Greave was already tense, but now fear started to come into it too. He knew what Aurelle would be shouting at him to do right now, and just the thought of that third option made him terrified. It wasn't just of the man in front of him, who was larger, stronger, and probably more dangerous. It was of the fact that he could even think like this.

"Face it," the other man said. "I'm going to Royalsport, and I'm going to tell them all that King Godwin's oh so lovely son is wandering around the kingdom, thinking that he can do something about the invasion. When they've finished laughing at the thought of *you* trying to stand up to them, maybe they'll come looking for you, or maybe they'll realize that it's just as easy to leave you out here, doing nothing."

"I can't let you go to Royalsport," Greave said. "There must be something I can offer you. When this is done ..."

"When this is done you'll be dead," Yan said to him. The big man stood. "You think you can do anything to stand up to King Ravin? Quiet Men will kill you before you get close, or soldiers, or both."

"I've faced soldiers," Greave said. "I was in Astare."

The big man sneered at that. "And you ... what? Ran away? Should I be impressed?"

Greave could sense which way this was going, and the problem with was that he'd already proved to himself that he couldn't do this.

"Please," Greave said, "just walk away. Go the way you were going."

"Look at you," Yan said. "Begging like a child. What kind of man does that? One of your brothers would have killed me by now. Your brother Rodry, I might even have followed him into battle. *He* might have been able to take this kingdom back."

"You know nothing about me," Greave said. He stood, matching the other man. "Or my family."

"I know that you've always been the weak one."

Greave tried one more thing. "How about you just give me a head start?" he suggested. "Stay out here for a week and then go to Royalsport. You can still get your coin from Ravin, say you passed me on the road. You can have my coin too. Everything you want, and I at least get time."

The big man actually paused, giving that thought. He shrugged. "You know what? I think King Ravin will pay me even more if I bring you to him. I've been thinking about it pretty much since we met the last time, cursing myself for running off rather than just grabbing you. Now … now I'm not so stupid as to give up a second chance."

Greave stood there. He knew he should probably run. He should plunge into the forest, get away from there, lose this man in the woods and hope to get to Royalsport ahead of him. Instead, he felt the weight of his eating knife in his hand. He couldn't even remember drawing it.

The other man laughed, drawing a knife of his own. "What do you think you're going to do with that? A prince who can barely hold a sword. A weakling. A—"

Greave stepped forward even while the other man was speaking, his knife slashing out the way Aurelle's might have, aiming for the throat. He felt the moment when the weapon cut through flesh, felt the warmth of the blood as it sprayed over his hand, heard the gasp of his opponent as the blade bit into his flesh.

His left hand went out to block the other man's own knife hand, stopping it before the weapon could get close to him. He held close to his opponent, caught there as the other man's eyes widened in shock and pain, the blood pumping from his veins. Because he'd read Xavis's *Dissections*, Greave knew exactly what was happening in the man's body as he died, the blood flowing away from the brain, the air unable to reach the lungs. Greave held onto him until his eyes glazed, and until he went from holding the other man back to holding him up. He heard his opponent's knife clatter to the ground.

He lowered the big man to the forest floor, staring down at him, feeling the weight of guilt settling on his shoulders. The man's dead eyes seemed to stare up at him accusingly, and Greave reached out to close them because he couldn't stand that stare.

"Why wouldn't you just take my money?" Greave demanded of the dead man.

He could imagine Aurelle telling him that he shouldn't care about any of this, that it was the thing that he'd had to do, and that even if this man had taken his money, Greave wouldn't have been able to trust him. Even so, Greave felt guilt running through him at the fact that he'd just killed a man.

The worst part was that he would have to kill plenty more before this was over. That thought made him swallow, and for a moment he let his knife go, to fall at his feet. He stood there for what seemed like forever, poised on the edge of what felt like running away, but then he knelt to scoop the knife up again, and his opponent's too. He wasn't the prince who was going to run away from this, whatever it took.

He took the man's cloak, wrapping it around his shoulders. He didn't stay there in the warmth of the campfire. Greave didn't feel like he deserved that. Instead, he turned and walked into the dark, setting off in the direction of the city.

CHAPTER TWENTY TWO

It was dark when Erin reached Royalsport. That was fine, because it made what she had to do so much easier. The only disadvantage was that it left no time to wait, to hole up and plan her approach or catch her breath, but Erin didn't need any of those things right then; she just needed Ravin dead.

Erin was cautious as she approached the slums outside the city. They might have no walls, but she wasn't stupid enough to think that they had no watchers. She padded silently through the muddy streets, keeping her grip tight on her spear.

There were a few more people out in the dark than there had been before, suggesting either that the curfew that had been in place had been relaxed, or that people were growing comfortable enough to know when they could get away with breaking it. Erin wasn't comfortable; she kept her eyes open for Quiet Men with every step.

There. In the shadows, she spotted a figure lurking, spying on a group. Erin slipped up close enough that she could see the insignia of Ravin's troops, the flash of red and purple in the shadows. Just the sight of it was enough to raise her anger, making her drive her spear into the back of the man's neck in one swift movement. The watcher crumpled without a sound.

Erin didn't bother hiding the body; if guards came to investigate, it would only draw them away from everywhere else. Even if they raised the alarm and locked down the castle, she wouldn't care. She would find a way through to do what she needed to do.

She made her way around to one of the smaller entrances to the city. It was open, but a light beyond suggested that it was watched. Erin considered her options. Maybe someone else would have come up with a cunning plan to gain entrance without being spotted, or just withdrawn and found another way, but Erin didn't have the patience for that. If there were men waiting beyond to question anyone who came through, she wasn't going to play the game of trying to talk her way past them.

She ran through the gate instead at full speed, and there were three guardsmen beyond, two of whom appeared to be playing cards while the third did the actual guarding. He moved to block Erin's path, and he died for it, her spear lancing out to plunge into his chest. Erin slammed into him, knocking him back, then kept running, plunging away into the dark before the other two could react enough to follow her. Shouting sounded behind Erin as she hurried on, but she ignored it, quickly leaving it behind.

She made her way to one of the rivers, and cursed her luck because now the tide was high, making it too dangerous to risk swimming, yet she knew that she couldn't chance any crossing the Southerners controlled. There, she really might be trapped, and even if she didn't fear dying doing this, she wouldn't do so without having completed her task.

That left Erin hunting around outbuildings and storehouses until she found what she wanted, in the form of a simple length of rope and a couple of iron bars that looked as though they might be bands waiting to be affixed to the outside of a chest. Erin tied them to either end of the rope and looked for a likely vantage point, finding a spot where two rooftops stood opposite one another with chimney stacks sticking up.

"It's no different than the night of the invasion," Erin whispered to herself as she swung the rope, flinging it out underhand, so that the iron briefly caught in the moonlight as it flew.

On the third attempt, she managed to get it to catch, but testing the strength of the hold quickly made it give way. It wasn't until the fifth try that she felt confident about how secure the rope was, and even then she took her time about securing her end.

Erin started out across the rope, using her spear as a balancing pole, stepping lightly as she ignored the rush of the river below. It might not be magically high now, but it was still fast enough that if she fell ... no, only cowards thought about falling. She just plunged forward, taking small, birdlike steps one after another until ...

There was an awful moment of stillness as Erin missed a step, feeling herself almost hang there teetering in the instant before she dropped. She started to fall, and her hand went out automatically, grabbing onto the rope hard enough that it jarred her shoulder. She almost lost her grip on her spear, but she clung to it as urgently as her life. She needed it to finish this.

Erin swung herself back up toward the rope, managed to catch it with her foot, and slowly scrambled across to the far side. She made it onto the far roof, jerked the rope free, and kept going.

Even in the night, the castle stood out against the rest of the city's skyline. Erin headed for it, working her way over the rooftops one by one, because it was the quickest way to avoid people below. She knew that she would have to descend at some point to cross the last part, but she needed to find the right spot.

When Erin saw two guards moving together below, she knew that she'd found her opportunity. She dropped on them, the weight of her slamming into the first of them, smashing the man to the ground. The impact of it made Erin's teeth rattle.

She recovered fast enough to strike up with her spear, skewering the guard who was still on his feet even as he tried to cry out. She stood and stabbed down, killing the guard she'd knocked over before he could recover. She ran again, moving forward in the dark even as she heard people converging on the spot where she'd been.

That was the point, and Erin smiled savagely in the moonlight as she heard a bell sounding an alarm back toward the walls where she'd come into the city. Every guard she drew away from the castle was one more who no longer stood between her and Ravin.

What *did* stand between her and him were the defenses of the castle. That meant the moat around the base, the walls, and then the strength of the keep's doors. For the moat, Erin took a simple approach, repeating her makeshift rooftop bridge, only this time she used her spear, flinging it hard into the ground on the far side, where it stuck quivering with the rope wrapped around the haft. She tied off her end, and this time she all but ran along the rope, wanting to leave no time to make a mistake.

When she reached the other side, Erin untied the rope from the spear and fastened it to the second piece of iron instead. With her spear across her back, she started to climb, her hands finding the smallest of cracks in the castle's walls. Her feet pushed as her hands pulled, raising her up little by little. Erin's muscles burned with it, and she felt as if her hands might give way, but she kept climbing in spite of that burn. When she got close to the top, she looked left and right until she was sure that there were no guards coming.

Finally, she slipped over the battlements, onto the wall. An army couldn't have done this. An army would have been seen, and Ravin had enough men to hold off the world here, in a way her family had not. Alone though, Erin could do this. She felt anticipation building along with the anger, and she kept going forward.

The most dangerous part was yet to come, because she still had to cross the space between the outer walls and the keep without being seen, and she still had to find a way into that keep once she got there. Erin didn't care about the danger, though, not when it came to this. She dropped lightly into the courtyard, sticking to the shadows as much as she could as she tried to make her way closer.

She froze as she heard the sound of booted feet approaching. Guards went past in formation, stomping off into the night while Erin pressed herself back against the wall, hoping that the shadows would hide her. She held her breath, willing them to go, not daring even the smallest twitch of movement until they passed.

The moment they did, though, she decided that she'd had enough of being cautious. The moonlight might make it obvious to anyone watching that she was approaching, but only if they happened to be looking the right way in that moment. Steeling herself, Erin sprinted across that space, not stopping until she was pressed in the shadows again, tight against the wall at the base of the keep.

Now what? The walls of the keep *might* be climbable, but doing it without being seen from the castle walls would be nearly impossible. No, she had to think of another way. The doors were her best option, but could she get through them without sounding the alarm? There would be at least two guards on a door like that, and if one of them managed to shout a warning here, it wouldn't be the help it had been in the city, because it would warn Ravin that she was coming.

Erin wasn't going to give in to fear, though, and besides, she had a plan. There was a spot not far from the door where she knew that a stone stuck out, providing plenty of opportunities to hide. Taking the butt of her spear, she hammered on that door, then slipped back into the shadows beneath the stone. The door opened a crack, then further as a guard poked his head out. Erin held her position, waiting.

"What's going on?" he demanded. "Who's there?"

He came out, sword drawn, and another man started to follow behind.

"Someone's out here," he said. "If this is some kind of joke, then know that the Quiet Men will kill you slow."

Erin kept waiting, and the men came out, looking for trouble. She heard them curse, and they went back inside. Erin waited a moment or two, then hammered on the door again. This time, she was barely back into her hiding place before the door opened again.

"That's it!" the first guard said. "I'm going to find you, and I'm going to kill you."

He and the other man came out, searching the area in front of the castle. Erin waited until their backs were turned and then slipped inside, through the still open door. Erin smiled to herself, proud of the way that she'd dealt with the two guards.

There was a third guard.

He stood staring at Erin, open-mouthed, and then turned as if he might run screaming into the depths of the keep.

Erin reacted on instinct, lifting her spear and flinging it, so that it sailed across the space between them to slam into the man's back. He stood for a moment transfixed, and then crumpled.

Erin breathed a sigh of relief as she walked to the guard and wrenched her spear free, then dragged his body back out of the way, where it wouldn't be noticed. She'd done it; she was inside. Now, she just needed to kill Ravin.

Chapter Twenty Three

There were, Renard decided, definitely some consolations to Meredith's "stay there and don't cause trouble" plan. One such consolation murmured in her sleep as he rose from the bed, while another opened her eyes, her tousled blonde hair falling in waves as she sat up with the covers clutched around her.

"Where are you going?" she asked. "Lady Meredith said that we were to keep you here by any means necessary."

That hurt Renard's pride a little, because he'd always done well enough with women, and hearing that these were here mostly to watch him stung just a touch.

"Oh, don't pout," the woman said. "You're perfectly lovely and you know it."

Renard *was* feeling more like himself now, and looking that way too. A glance in the room's mirror told him that his hair had returned to its usual fiery red, and his skin looked healthy again, not pallid and lined as it had been. As for his energy ... well, he felt that he'd proved that to the satisfaction of everyone concerned in the last little while.

"Pity Meredith can't be here," he said.

"She had other matters to attend to." The woman patted the bed beside her. "Come back here."

"Let me go fetch wine first," Renard said. Meredith might have instructed him to stay there, but that didn't mean that Renard was literally going to stay in one room. Pushing at the edges of other people's rules was one of the things he did best.

Finding his clothes, he headed down into the main body of the House. There were plenty of people there, of course, because there were *always* plenty of people there, some wearing masks and costumes, some not wearing very much at all, although it was less common outside of private rooms. Renard found a bottle of wine, opened it with his teeth, and took a swig. It felt good to be alive, or at least not to slowly have the life being drained out of him by the amulet.

It felt good enough that when he saw a lute in one corner, Renard actually took it up and started to play. He started with "The Chamberlain's Hands" because here of all places a bit of bawdiness would always go down well, but somehow he found the tune turning more maudlin, with the haunting minor tones of "Planxty for Lady Mirren" spilling out. For the first time in a long time, Renard actually felt happy. Maybe when all this was done, he could stay here and sing for his supper.

He was still playing when he saw the old man in the tattered dark robes enter the room. It wasn't that there were no old men who visited the House of Sighs, plenty did, and at least some of them looked like washed up scholars from *that* House. Very few of them, however, were likely to wander in vaguely, holding a strange contraption made from twigs as if it were precious. Renard saw him shake it with a frown, then cough pointedly in a way that somehow made all the noise and bustle of the House of Sighs stop around him.

"Sorry to interrupt," the old man said. "But I don't suppose anyone here has seen an amulet somewhere here? It would be octagonal, set with stones. Anyone?"

Renard frowned at that. He almost spoke up, but then he thought of the kind of people who might be searching for something like this. Was this man some kind of agent for the Hidden?

"Who are you, old man?" one of the masked patrons of the House demanded. "Why are you interrupting our evening?"

"I told you what I'm looking for," the old man said. "As for who I am, isn't it obvious?"

"No."

The old man stood there for a moment, and even though nothing seemed to change about him in that moment, everything did. It was as if power radiated from him, and authority, so that everyone in the room took a step back. A second after that, his robes shifted their color, becoming a pure white, edged with gold.

"You ... you're the king's sorcerer," Renard said.

The old man nodded solemnly. "And you know more than you are saying."

Renard swallowed. He'd had the Hidden look into his eyes, with all their terrible power, and all the madness that it had brought in them, but somehow this old man seemed to look right through him.

"I know where what you're looking for is," he said.

"Show me."

Renard led the way, and as he did so, he felt a sense of relief seep through him. In just a minute or two, he would be rid of the amulet. He would give it to the sorcerer, and he wouldn't have to worry about it again. For once, just once, it seemed to Renard that the gods weren't making his life worse just for their amusement.

Renard reached his room and found that the women there were already gone. Ah well, they probably had other things to do with the House so busy. Renard gestured vaguely.

"Take a seat."

He saw Master Grey look round and stay standing. Renard went over to his hiding place, lifting the rug, then the floorboard.

"Who are you?" Master Grey asked. "How do you come to have the amulet?"

"I'm Renard. I'm a ... thief." It was probably better to be honest. "Some people persuaded me to fetch it for them."

Glancing back, he thought he saw Master Grey frown.

"What is it?" Renard asked.

"I fear that we may not be talking about the same amulet. If you had touched it ..."

Renard didn't want the wizard deciding to back out of this, not when he was so close to finally getting rid of the amulet. He took out the box he'd put it in, opened it quickly, and took out the amulet to show the sorcerer. Instantly, he felt the faint pull on his life, but now at least he had some strength to spare.

"Here," Renard said, holding it out to Master Grey. "Is this, or is this not, what you're looking for?"

The magus was very quiet for a moment, looking at the amulet, then at Renard.

"That is ... impressive," Master Grey said. He made no move to touch the amulet. "You realize, of course, that you should be dead."

He sounded surprised that Renard wasn't, and from his reluctance to touch what Renard held, being a sorcerer wasn't a protection from it. That shouldn't have come as a surprise to Renard, though; the Hidden had sent him for it rather than fetching it themselves for a reason.

"I came to Royalsport to try to get rid of this," Renard said. "I've seen what happens when other people touch it. I can *feel* what it's doing to me. I thought a sorcerer would be able to help me. Now, you're looking for this amulet. So if you want to take it off my hands, be my guest."

"It is not so simple," Master Grey said. "You know what it can do to the unprotected. It will also attract unwanted attention."

"From dragons," Renard said, and Master Grey stopped short, staring at him. "I had to throw myself over a waterfall to avoid one, back in Geertstown."

"Then you know the scale of the danger that could come," Master Grey said.

"So don't take it," Renard said. "Destroy it."

"To do so would be to take away our most vital weapon in what is to come," Master Grey said. "You have seen one dragon. Now imagine hundreds and the amulet the only thing that stands between us and them. No, I will take the amulet, but to do that, *you* must help me to get it to somewhere I can contain it, so that others will not be able to sense it."

"And where is that?" Renard asked. Just when he'd thought that his luck was starting to turn.

"There is an apparatus within my tower that will do it," Master Grey said.

"Your tower? Surrounded by King Ravin's troops?" Ravin sighed. He should have known better than to think anything could ever be *simple* for him.

"Don't frown so," Master Grey said. "I thought you said that you were a thief. Presumably a good one if you were contracted to steal something of such importance."

"The best," Renard said, before he could stop himself.

"Then you should have no problem getting us there." Master Grey stood by the door expectantly.

"The thing is," Renard tried, "I'm really supposed to stay here. Meredith herself told me to."

"And which of us are you more worried by, right now?" the magus asked.

Frankly, it was a close run thing. The trouble was though, if he didn't go with Master Grey, Renard would probably never be free of the amulet. He would be stuck there with it under the House of Sighs' floorboards forever. He had to at least try.

"All right," he said. "Then we'd better go now, before Meredith gets back."

Renard grabbed his sword and his cloak, tucked away the amulet in a belt pouch, and then they set off, making their way down through the House of Sighs and out into the city.

Renard picked the way, skulking along with all the skill and silence of his profession, choosing a route that would avoid guards. Master Grey was back to looking like just an old scholar, but he walked quite calmly in Renard's wake, strolling along without worry, as if certain that nothing bad would happen.

It just went to show that even wizards got to be wrong sometimes.

They were halfway through the noble district when three figures stepped out in front of them, one coming each from alleys to the left and right, while another approached from in front, the darkness of his robes rendering him all but invisible against the night. It was only when he got closer that Renard could make out the pale blankness of the mask beneath, the pits of emptiness that were his eyes. The figure from the left walked in a trail of flowers blooming up from under the cobbles hard enough to crack them, while the one from the right thrust one fist into a wall as he passed, shattering the brick in an obvious display of power.

Verdant, Wrath, and Void stood in front of Renard, and he felt the gathering of their power. Or maybe it was his own fear; it was kind of hard to tell the difference right then. Renard was so certain that he'd left the Hidden behind, and now here they were again. He looked around for a way out, but there was none.

Void held out a hand. "Give us what's ours, and I will at least kill you quick."

Chapter Twenty Four

As the evening closed in, Devin sat in his parents' house with Sigil, thinking of all that he had lost. He sat at the rough wood of the kitchen table, a bowl of beef broth in front of him, but with no appetite to eat it. The emptiness of the house seemed almost to taunt him, leaving too much space where before there had been almost none.

"It's just you and me, Sigil," he said, setting the bowl on the floor and running a hand through the wolf's fur. Sigil started to lap at the broth hungrily.

The people he had called his parents had not been *good* parents, had not even wanted to be his parents if the things his father had said were true. They had often been harsh, and had rejected him in the end, yet nothing about grief was neat, or logical. It didn't matter to Devin what they'd been like; only that they were gone.

There were other, sharper, griefs too. Devin's thoughts turned to Lenore, as they had so many times now. He couldn't believe that she was gone, just like that. He couldn't believe that in the short time that Devin had been away, searching for the components of the Unfinished Sword, she had been snatched from the world by Emperor Ravin's cruelty.

From him. There, now that she was gone, Devin could admit how much he had loved her, and how much he had hoped that somehow things could work out between them. Instead, he'd been sent away by Master Grey, and now Lenore was dead. The pain of that felt like a mist obscuring everything else, making it hard to see past it to the world.

Had the magus known what would happen? Every instinct Devin had said that he must have. It wasn't just that Master Grey always seemed to know what was going on, or that he'd spoken about prophecies with such certainty when it came to Devin; it was the fact that he'd sent Devin away to find the sword right at the crucial moment, told him that *his* role was to find it, rather than to be a part of the war against the Southern Kingdom.

Of course, with a sorcerer, it was hard to tell what was coincidence and what was intended. Master Grey had never been one to explain himself, and even now, Nem had said that he was gone, missing sometime after his magic during the invasion.

Devin thought about that magic and reached out for Sigil. He could *feel* the flow of magic now, seeing the world so much more clearly than he had before. Even without Sigil he could see some of it, but with the wolf as a conduit, he could do so much more. He'd stilled storms and lit fires with this power within him, finding the balancing points in the world so that the small touches of magic he could produce could have greater effects. If he'd been there during the attack ...

Devin sighed and stood, letting go of his contact with Sigil. If he'd been there during the attack, he wouldn't have *had* this knowledge, and he would have been useless. That was the awful thing, the thing he'd been going over again and again in his head. Devin couldn't think of a way where he could have still been in Royalsport *and* have the power to save Lenore. The impossibility of it just made him feel helpless, and the fact that he'd accomplished the mission Master Grey had sent him on was no consolation at all.

"All this, just for a sword," Devin said to Sigil.

He went over to the spot at the side of the room where the Unfinished Sword sat, still wrapped in the layers of cloth that had let Devin carry it through the city without attracting attention. He set that bundle down on the table and unwrapped it, letting the sword out into the light.

It wasn't finished, even now. The blade was complete and perfect, but it still needed the crosspiece of the hilt putting in place, a grip attaching, and a pommel. Even so, there was something beautiful about it, with the runes Devin had worked into the surface catching the light as they balanced the competing strands of magic within it. Devin lifted the sword, thinking of all the hours it had taken to get it this far. A part of him wanted to snap it, just so that it matched the way he felt inside. More of him wanted to finish it though, so that he would have something he could ram through the heart of the man who had killed Lenore.

What would he need for this? Not a forge for this part, thankfully, because getting one without soldiers asking questions would be impossible. He would need materials, and some way to affix them, that was all. The question was what was right.

Devin set off from the house, leaving Sigil there because it would still attract far too much attention to walk the city with a wolf beside him. Around him, the poor part of the city felt quiet and tense. People left their houses and hurried about their business, not stopping to talk, keeping apart from one another as if afraid that being seen together might lead to Quiet Men listening in. Probably here, there was nothing for Quiet Men to listen to, and they had no interest in doing so, but people were being cautious nonetheless. The new regime didn't need a watcher on every corner when they could have that presence in people's minds.

Devin scoured the streets, darting into back alleys, looking for what he needed. He found some of what he needed when he saw a tree so old that it could have been there before the city, the wood silvery and solid. Devin found a fallen branch, the wood dried out and thick enough for what he needed.

He found another part of it in the form of a discarded copper pan. Devin might not have a forge, but using the clay-heavy soil of the district, he could make a simple structure to melt this and cast it in the shape he wanted for a hilt. He found a discarded leather boot with a hole in the sole, and a lump of amber wedged randomly behind a barrel.

They were small things, simple things, things he hadn't had to travel the length of a kingdom to fetch. The rest of the sword was a thing of powerful, magical metal, but Devin wanted the finishing of it to be simpler. He wanted it to be a thing finished with the elements of home.

He took them back to the house. The hilt was the first part of it, and Devin made that by molding the shape out of wax, then covering it with clay until it was a block that would hold together, leaving a hole at either end. He melted down the copper in a great iron cauldron that his mother had used for cooking, then poured it into the dried out block of the clay, so that the wax poured out from the other end of it.

He worked on the wood for the grip while he waited for it to cool. Devin whittled at it with a small knife, pulling in threads of magic as he did, pinning that magic in place with scratches of the tip even as he shaped it to fit human hands. He deliberately kept the grip long, so that it could be wielded with one hand or two, and knew that he would have to adjust the balance of the pommel to make sure that it was all perfect.

When the copper of the hilt was cool, Devin broke open the clay to remove it. He had enough tools to file the rough edges down, and even then it was possible to work more magic into it, working in hints of stability and protection, using a chisel and a hammer to stamp in the lines as he traced the flow of the magic.

Devin fit the hilt next, heating the tang of the sword and then driving it down into the wood so that it burned its way through, the fit tighter than it could ever have been if he'd drilled it out.

For the pommel, Devin did things differently. He reached out for Sigil's fur then so that he would have the extra connection to the flow of the magic, and took the lump of amber, feeling the way it fit together, the way there was something still living about it even though it was something so old and preserved. Devin dove down into the way it fit together, into the sensation of that life within it. He touched that life with his magic, encouraging it and building on it so that he started to feel the amber flow under his fingers.

He shaped it, fitting it to the end of the tang, locking the rest of the assembly into place. He thought of the energies balanced within the blade, life and death, fire and ice, so that the amber formed a sphere of swirling colors, every shift in angle seeming to make it glow in a different way.

Devin set the sword down on the table. It was no longer unfinished; instead, it was … it was perfect. Devin could feel the magic singing within it, the parts somehow greater than the whole. There was only one thing missing from it: a name. A sword like this needed a name, because names had a power of their own, and gave things purpose.

He thought about all the things that had happened while he was gone, and he took up the blade, sending flickers of magic into the star metal at the base of the blade, so that letters formed there, just above the hilt.

Loss.

It was the only name to give it, and with luck, it would be the blade he used to take back some of what was lost. Devin lifted the blade and swung it, feeling the perfection of its balance. He tossed an apple into the air and cut, the sharpness of the blade slicing through it in one clean movement.

He was still practicing with it when he heard Sigil growl. Devin frowned, watching the wolf as Sigil stared at the door. He knew enough to trust the wolf's senses, so he moved to the door carefully, the sword still in his hand. He swung the door open, not willing to wait while someone sneaked around, and looked out into the dark.

He saw a figure there, approaching the house slowly, and surprise flooded through Devin, because he recognized that man, with his dark leathers, his short blond hair strung with charms, and his wild look. The man who had sent him to Royalsport stared back at Devin, and now Devin was sure that he wasn't just a messenger. This was about more, much more. The man stepped forward, approaching the door openly now, and he held out a hand.

"I've come for the sword."

Chapter Twenty Five

The only advantage that Grey had in the face of the Hidden was that they didn't know who he was. It didn't feel like much of an advantage. They stood there in front of him, Void with his hand outstretched, the others at his side, and for the first time in a long time, Grey knew fear.

He knew their names, knew what they could do, and the price they'd paid for it. Their magic was wild and powerful and direct, while for him to balance the forces needed to produce great effects took time. Against one, it might be enough to just strike once, but three... three was a dangerous challenge.

If he could get to his tower, things might be different, but the tower was still a little way away, the castle across the noble district.

"Give us the amulet," Void repeated, and Grey saw Renard take a step back. He could understand the desire to do so. Right then, even Grey felt like running.

Grey checked himself. Was he not still the finest magus ever to walk this kingdom? Had he not done more with magic than any man before him? The Hidden might have traded themselves for power, but they had it over only one field. The connections between all things that *real* magic was built on eluded them.

"*Could* I give it to them?" Renard asked, with a glance to Grey. Grey knew what he was asking. If the amulet had killed so many before, then maybe it would kill them too. Grey wished it were as simple as that.

"They probably have a way to contain its energies set up," Grey said. "Even if they don't, the thought of giving them that much power even for a few instants... we can't."

"Who's your friend?" Verdant asked, looking over at Grey, even though her words were intended for Renard. She took a step closer, almost close enough to touch him. "He seems...expendable. Maybe if we remind you of what we can do, you'll be more inclined to cooperate."

Grey felt the moment when she reached out with her magic, felt the rush of green things growing, tasted the scent of jungle blooms. Thorny tendrils broke up through the ground, reaching for him to tear him apart.

Grey took hold of that magic, because while the Hidden might have power, *he* was the one with control. He turned it back toward Verdant, and she barely leapt aside as the tendrils grabbed at her.

"Who *are* you?" Verdant demanded.

Grey drew power into himself, as much as he could hold. Normally, this wasn't the way he worked with magic, but this was no time for subtlety. He shone with power, at least to those with the eyes to see it. He let the illusion that had shifted the colors of his robe and his appearance fall, letting them see him exactly as he was.

"The king's sorcerer," Void said. "The amulet *and* the chance to kill you? The world is too kind."

"Your power really *has* twisted your mind if you think that you can best me," Grey said, but even as he said it, Wrath raised his hands beside Void and sent a blast of power Grey's way. This time Grey could not deflect it completely, but he could change it, using the power involved to create a gust of wind that knocked Renard away from him. The thief went sprawling, rolled, and came up to his feet again.

"When the chance comes, run, Renard," Grey said. "Do not look back." He sent a flicker of power around the amulet. "This spell should hide it from their attempts to track it for a brief while."

One good thing about a man like that: he didn't need to be told twice to run. Grey saw him poised to do it, and turned his full attention to the advancing Hidden. He would need it, and more, if he was going to defeat them.

"This does not have to end in violence," Grey said. "You could walk away now, and accept that there is no profit in this for you."

"Or you could step aside and let us have the amulet," Void said.

"It is needed for what is to come."

"Yes," Void agreed. "Then it seems we get to finish this."

Grey felt the moment when the other man reached for the depths of his magic, felt the crushing weight of despair start to turn into a sharp-edged agony within him, powerful enough to get past even his defenses. In the same moment, Grey finished the last strands of a spell he'd been weaving all the time that he'd been talking. Taking a small bead, he flung it, and his spell gave it force and weight beyond anything that it should have possessed. Had it struck home, it would have crushed Void like a stone from a catapult. Instead, Grey saw the three Hidden work together to shield their leader, Wrath taking control of the stone while Verdant produced a shield of vines behind it, and Void swallowed the power with the raw emptiness that seemed to sit behind his mask.

They struck back, and it was all Grey could do to survive. Wrath gestured to the wall of a house near Grey, and the magus had to fling himself aside as it toppled toward him. Plants burst around him in clouds of noxious fumes. Shards of pure entropy came for his head.

He threw himself around a corner, just for a moment's respite from the onslaught, but the Hidden followed him. Grey set the wind howling among lines of washing turning the lines into lashing, cutting whips, but all that could do was slow the Hidden, not stop them. Void raised his hands and the washing turned aged and ashen, finally tumbling to the ground as it disintegrated.

Of all of them, he was the most dangerous, and not just because he was the one of them who was holding the madness brought on by power in check the best. Grey hadn't known that he had grown as powerful as this, that any of them had.

In his younger days, perhaps Grey would have fought a running battle with them, flinging bursts of power and running, staying secure until he could find an opening to strike back. Even as it was, he managed to take a wave of flame that Wrath was going to fling and twist it so that it consumed thorn-covered vines that were starting to pour from Verdant's hands. A flicker of that flame caught the woman and she yelped in pain.

She and Wrath continued to pour in with their attacks, whispering madness set against pure violence as they came in from either side. Grey fought and moved, heading in the direction of the castle, trying to get to the tools there that might aid him in the fight.

Tempting whispers sounded in Grey's ears, and he ignored them. The stones at his feet cracked, and he jumped back. He sent a spray of poison away to strike a wall, deflected a charge by Wrath using spray from a kicked up puddle amplified until it became a wave.

He dealt with attack after attack by the pair, and now it seemed that he was getting closer to the castle, to his tower, to safety. It was only after the dozenth such deflection that he thought to ask himself why Void was holding back.

He realized the danger a second too late, as the leader of the Hidden unleashed a spell that he'd obviously been building in the seconds before. A web of dark power settle around Grey, crushing in and holding him, making it impossible to move without touching the energy of it. Worse, that energy was contracting, constricting.

In that moment, Grey realized just how badly he had underestimated the Hidden. He'd thought of them as just more of those who dabbled in magic, who took shortcuts rather than trying to understand things, and who could never hope to be on the same level as a fully trained magus. Yet Void's spell had subtlety to it, and complexity. It wasn't some piece-meal weaving that Grey could just unravel with a thought, and in the time it *would* take to escape, he was sure that the other Hidden would be more than able to strike him down. A second thought came to Grey then, and a terrifying one:

After all these years, he was actually going to die.

There had been times when he was younger that he had felt this way, facing horrors that most people wouldn't even begin to understand. For the longest time though, he had been secure in the thought that he knew what was coming, and that he was more than strong enough to deal with everything in the meantime. Now, it seemed that he was wrong.

"For so long," Void said, stepping forward, "I heard stories of the king's sorcerer. I heard how he was a greater magus than any man before had been. I heard the tales of the monsters he had defeated, the knowledge he had learned. Yet look at you now, caught and at my mercy."

He had no options left, no way out. Except one.

"Your power is tainted," Grey said, thinking all the while. Magic was volatile, hard to contain. If he set all of his free, tangling with that of the Hidden, the destruction that would result would be massive. It would destroy all three of the Hidden, probably along with quite a lot of the nearby castle walls. There was only one problem with it ... it would kill him too.

"My power is *real*," Void said, "while yours is a sham of small touches, made to seem larger than they are. And my power will grow more still when we have the amulet."

Grey knew in that moment that he had to do it. He had to kill the Hidden before they got the amulet, even if it meant the end of him after so very long. He started to reach deep into his power, started to feel for the power of the others, and to link the two, binding them so that when he unraveled his own magic, theirs would unravel with it. The sudden release of power would form a blast that would probably level most of the street, but to be rid of the Hidden, he was prepared to do it.

"If I had more time," Void said, "I would wring your mind dry. I would claim every secret within it, before I destroyed you. As it is, I will have to settle for your death."

This was it, the moment when Grey would have to do it. He wasn't ready, but then, he found that he'd never been ready, no matter how long his life had gone on. His magic had sustained him longer than any man could hope, but even so it felt like too soon. Despite that, he reached down into himself, ready to tear everything asunder.

That was when the roar came thundering over the houses around Grey, loud enough to rattle windows in their frames. Grey saw the one shape that he had been hoping never to see in the skies of the Northern Kingdom again rise over a roof, its scales blue and shining, its mouth open to let out a gout of flame.

The dragon swooped, and Grey didn't know whether he was about to be saved or burned alive.

CHAPTER TWENTY SIX

Erin moved up through the keep, keeping to the shadows as she headed for the rooms that had once been her father's. She'd spent so much of her childhood wandering these halls, running as she played with her siblings, hiding from her mother's attempts to make her dress like a proper princess.

Now, she used every nook and cranny of the keep to stay out of sight. It wasn't what she *wanted* to do, though. She wanted to charge through this keep, killing anyone who got in her way. That way, though, there was too much of a chance that her prey would get away from her, so she kept padding forward on silent feet, heading ever upward.

When she emerged on the top floor of the keep, Erin saw the doors of her father's old rooms ahead. Guards stood there, leaning on halberds. Erin readied herself to throw herself at them, but the sound of the door opening made her pause, pressing herself into a niche while she waited to see what was happening.

A woman came out, a servant by the look of her, a tangle of emotions etched on her face as she hurried from the room. One of the guards took her by the elbow, and Erin saw her flinch.

That was when Erin struck. Taking out a dagger, she threw it, tumbling end over end until it slammed point first into the guard's throat. Even as it was in the air, she was running forward, leading with her spear, sheer momentum carrying it through the other guard's chest. She let go of it and spun to the woman, managing to get a hand across her mouth before she could cry out in shock.

"Don't make a sound," Erin said. "I'm not going to hurt you."

She slowly took her hand away.

"Do you know who I am?"

"Yes," the serving woman breathed.

"Then you know what I'm going to do here," Erin said.

She nodded.

"Better if you're not around when that happens." Erin gestured to the stairs. "Go."

She gave the woman a few moments to escape before she pushed the door open in silence. She padded through the chambers there, taking in the ways that Ravin had changed things. Statues of him stood at each corner of the first room, while the furniture she knew had been swapped for curved and whorled couches in the southern style.

The bedroom lay ahead. She knew from experience of sneaking into her father's chambers as a girl that there was a moment when it creaked, but she also knew that holding it just *so* stopped the sound.

She slipped into the near darkness of the room beyond, the moon through the windows providing the only light. By that light, Erin could see the things that had changed, a suit of armor set on a stand in one corner, a great two-handed sword set against it. A bed sat at the far side of the room, and Erin's heart pounded as she saw Ravin lying on it, clad in a purple robe.

She waited, making sure that he was asleep before she took the first step into the room. She could feel her anger building inside her, but also her anticipation. She was there. She could end this, once and for all.

Erin padded across the room, her spear ready as she moved into place, next to the bed. She looked down at Ravin, watching him sleep for a second and thinking of all that he had done to hurt her and her family. She took deep breaths, lifting her spear, wanting to savor this moment, not wanting to forget a single instant of it as she prepared to drive the spear down into Ravin's heart.

One thrust would be all it would take. One thrust and this would be over. One thrust, and Erin would have revenge for all of them. She tightened her grip on the spear.

Below her, Ravin opened his eyes.

Erin thrust down with a cry, but the emperor was already rolling out of the way. Erin felt her spear slam down into the mattress, cutting

130

through it easily as she dragged it clear. Erin let out another cry, this one of frustration.

"How did you get in here?" Ravin demanded. He sprang toward the armor stand in the corner. Erin moved to block his way, stabbing out with her spear again, but the emperor threw himself into a roll so that her spear passed over his head. His foot lashed out, catching her in the stomach and knocking her a step back.

Even as Erin recovered her balance, she saw him snatch up his sword, holding it in both hands, raised overhead, ready to cut down the moment she approached. If he'd been moving in panic a second ago, now he was poised, dangerous, deadly.

"I take it there's no point in trying to call for my guards?" he said.

"They're dead," Erin said. She hefted her spear, trying to judge the distance between them, letting her anger rise up inside her. "You're next."

"Try," Ravin said, with a taunting smile.

Erin let all the anger she'd been holding back pour out in that moment, charging in toward Ravin. She wasn't stupid though, and she flung herself to one side at the last moment, deflecting the downward cut that would otherwise have slammed into her shoulder and chest.

She thrust at Ravin and he parried, her spear tangling with his blade. The emperor tried to wind the weapon from her hands, but Erin was fast enough to disengage her spear from his blade, getting a blow in with the butt that earned a grunt of pain from Ravin.

He cut back at her, feinting high and going low. Erin saw it easily and leapt over the blow, then cursed as that turned out to be only a second feint. Ravin thrust for her while she was still in midair. With no time to dodge, Erin did her best to deflect the blow, but it slid past her spear anyway. Only her armor stopped it from skewering her completely, but even so the blade slid along her flesh, opening a wound that felt like a line of fire.

"Weak," Ravin said, dismissing her with a single word.

Erin let out a roar of fury, striking at him again and again. Her spear head was everywhere at once, moving with all the speed that her anger lent her. Ravin blocked most of those blows, but Erin managed to get in a cut that scraped across his arm, a thrust that grazed his side as he turned from it.

Most men would have fallen back under the weight of that attack, but Ravin came forward instead, meeting Erin's fury with his own calculating anger, cut after cut coming her way. One struck her arms, battering them even through her armor. A kick struck her in the guts, almost knocking her to the ground. Erin barely kept the emperor away from her by thrusting up toward Ravin's throat. Even so, the tip of his sword scraped across her back, opening up more pain.

She managed to get in another cut against the emperor, this one a wound to the thigh. Even as she struck, Erin saw that the opening was a trap. Ravin was actually cold enough to let himself be wounded to open up an opportunity. As her spear sank into his flesh, he cut down, striking the haft of it behind its head, cutting through the wood of it in one clean movement.

Erin stared in horror at the short length of wood in her hand. The weapon had been hers, designed for her alone, and now all that she had to fight with was the haft. She barely deflected the next blow that Ravin sent her way, dove out of the way of an overhand cut that slammed into the ground where she had been with the ringing sound of steel on stone. Erin reached for her knife, then cursed herself as she realized that she hadn't retrieved it from the throat of the guard she'd killed with it.

She gave ground as Ravin came forward. The wound that she'd inflicted on his thigh slowed him enough that she could dodge the first swinging cuts, but her own wounds hurt, and Erin could feel herself slowing down.

Ravin raised his sword for another cut and Erin threw herself forward in desperation, grabbing hold of his arms and the grip of his sword, trying to stop the weapon from cutting into her. She grappled with Ravin at close range, and the moment she started to do so, Erin knew it was a mistake. He was so much stronger than her that instantly, she found herself being pressured back, her body being twisted over off balance. She struck out at Ravin with her knees and feet and hands, but every time she let go to do it, she found the sword growing closer to her.

He hit her, striking out with a knee that thudded into her stomach, the pain of it sickening and debilitating. He struck again, and now it was like

Erin's body was refusing to do what she wanted. She fell to one knee, and a third blow from Ravin slammed into her jaw.

The world swam around her, and now Erin was on her back, without any real memory of the seconds that had brought her there. She felt dull impacts as Ravin kicked her again and again. She tasted blood in her mouth, and pain wrapped around her like a blanket.

Ravin was standing over her now, blood darkening the robe that he wore in the spots where Erin had wounded him. He stared down at her with something surprising: respect.

"You fought well," he said. "But not well enough. I'm going to find your sister. I'm going to kill her. I'm going to wipe away every trace of your family from this kingdom. But you won't see it."

He started to lift the sword he held. In the moonlight, Erin could see the blood on it, and she was so dizzy that it was hard to remember that it was her blood. She couldn't move now, couldn't do anything about it as it lifted, and she knew that when Ravin brought it down, she was going to die.

CHAPTER TWENTY SEVEN

Ravin stood over the defeated form of his foe, drinking in the moment as he prepared to deliver the killing blow. Most of the time, he played the part of the calm and calculating ruler, but in moments like this, it was impossible not to feel satisfaction singing through his body, the sense of triumph building in him as he raised his sword for the stroke that would end her...

Light burst over the city, and a rumble of sound like thunder, only a hundred times louder. An explosion sounded outside, and the rumble of it was enough to throw Ravin off balance, the flash of it half blinding him, leaving after-images stinging his eyes. Outside, Ravin heard alarms sounding, people shouting, the sounds of a terrified response from his guards.

He ran to the window, looking out, trying to make sense of the sudden blinding light. More flashes came, accompanied by more explosions, each one large enough that Ravin felt it like a rumble through his bones. There were moments in those seconds when it seemed as if the air itself were on fire. The city certainly was, flames licking up from the fringes of the noble district, houses turned into pillars of flame by some inexplicable force.

What was happening? Was this some kind of attack? Had the princess's assassination attempt merely been the first move in some kind of fight to retake the city? Were these flashes down to some new siege engine that even Ravin hadn't heard of, or had the old king's sorcerer found a more direct kind of magic than raising rivers and disappearing suddenly? Ravin didn't know, and not knowing scared him in a way that most foes could not.

In the next flash, Ravin saw it.

The bulk of the dragon hung over the city, blue-scaled and leathery, bursts of energy flying around it as someone did battle with it using what could only be magic to try to bring it down. Even as Ravin watched, it opened its mouth and flame lanced out in response, striking the houses below it and sending them up in a cascade of fire.

There was something primal and terrifying about the sight of it there. Ravin had faced many foes, both human and beast. He had fought men in single combat and survived countless would-be assassins. He had stood in the middle of battles with his heart cold as stone as he shouted orders, yet there was something about the sight of the beast there that meant that he could only stare at it for long seconds.

"No," he managed after a moment. "It can't be ... they ... there hasn't been a dragon here in *lifetimes*."

Yet there it was, swooping over the city, so close to the walls that Ravin could make out the details of its scales every time it blew fiery breath down toward its targets on the ground. It circled, as if hunting for something, then dove again, a fresh line of flame scouring the city below.

Even as he stared at it, Ravin knew that he had to do something. Below, he could see men running around the castle, trying to work out what to do, and it was in moments like this that a king had to be seen, had to make the decisions that mattered. Ravin was no coward king like Vars; he would not stand back here and let others make the choices that mattered with *his* castle under attack.

He spun back toward the princess, recovering a sense of himself long enough to realize that he should finish what he'd started with her. A quick thrust, and then ...

When he turned, though, there was an empty space where she had been lying on the floor of his chambers. A smear of blood showed the direction in which she had fled, and on another day, Ravin would have hunted her down slowly, playing cat and mouse until he caught and killed her.

The roar of the dragon outside reminded him that he had no time to start pursuing one princess. Instead, Ravin ran to his armor, pulling the most important pieces of it into place and trying to ignore the pain of his wounds. The girl had come closer than most to ending him.

Now that he was armored, Ravin ran from his rooms, heading down the stairs beyond and moving through the keep. Men were waiting for him, joining him so that it seemed that he was a comet pulling a tail of advisors along behind him. A commander among the Quiet Men fell into step with him, and a captain of the guards, but there were noblemen too, and servants. Even Lord Finnal was there, still dressed in his night things, yet clutching that oh so fancy sword of his as if he might take the dragon on himself.

"What are we going to do?" a nobleman demanded, sounding on the verge of panic. "What is anyone supposed to do against a *dragon*?"

Ravin turned and struck the man, hard enough to send him sprawling. "You will do what you are commanded to do. Now, follow."

He led the way to the great hall. Already, it was packed with people. Nobles and soldiers, servants and seemingly all the others of the castle were there, waiting for instructions. Ravin strode to the front of them, feeling their attention upon him. He kept his face from showing any of the myriad of emotions he felt, keeping his expression determined and focused. People needed to see an emperor who was in control, in command.

That meant *giving* commands and thankfully, Ravin already knew the commands that he wanted to give.

"Archers to the walls," he said. "Every soldier and Quiet Man who can hold a bow is to take one from the armory and use it. If that thing comes close, I want it peppered with shafts."

"Will arrows stop a *dragon*?" a soldier asked. "In the stories—"

"I don't *care* about stories!" Ravin bellowed. "If it breathes, it can be killed, and arrows will stop even a man in armor. Are you going to try to tell me that a dragon's scales are thicker than plate?"

None of them dared to. Distantly, Ravin remembered a few stories about dragons from his childhood, from the rare occasions when he hadn't been plotting his rise among his father's sons and the nobles of the Southern Kingdom. There had been stories of men bringing such beasts down, heroes slaying them, so it had to be possible, didn't it?

"I see men from this city's House of Scholars here," Ravin said, picking out a few of the black robes among the rest of those there. "You will consult your books, and you will tell me *everything* that is known about dragons before the dawn, or I will have your heads."

He saw some of the men there flinch, presumably thinking of how little they knew about dragons. Ravin didn't care. If men of knowledge could not give him the knowledge that he wanted, then what use were they?

He addressed the rest of them then. "The castle is strong," he said. "It is made of stone, and stone does not burn the way wood and thatch do. We will ride out the attack here, driving the beast off with arrows. I want men to go and close the gates."

"The gates, my emperor?" To Ravin's surprise, that came from Lord Finnal, who looked uncomfortable at the prospect. "Gates will not keep out a dragon, when it can burn them, or simply fly."

"But they *will* keep out the panicked hordes of city folk who might otherwise come into this castle, demanding safety and overwhelming us all," Ravin said. "They will keep out those whose very presence might make it harder to defend this space. They will prevent panic, and will mean that the dragon will *have* to fly if it wants to enter the castle, so that the archers have a better chance of driving it off."

Ravin was not used to explaining himself. He gave commands, and people obeyed. Those who did not tended to die horribly. He explained his reasoning now for two reasons. First, it reassured the people there that their emperor had the situation fully under control. Second, Finnal and his father were among the more powerful nobles of the kingdom, and their support had been of use in ensuring that there was no serious revolt against his conquest.

"Shut the gates," Ravin repeated. "Let no one in or out."

To his shock, though, Finnal spoke again. "Emperor Ravin, my father is out in the city, in one of our town houses there. He had business to attend to. Surely you do not mean to deny *him* the protection of the castle?"

Ravin strode over to the young nobleman, giving him the full weight of the stare that had made enemies back away and caused commanders to surrender rather than face his forces. He drew himself up to his full height, just one short step away from striking out with his sword.

"You and your father have been useful to me," Ravin said in a carefully controlled voice. "Your quick submission to my rule meant that a lot of men who might have tried to stand and fight chose to kneel as well. Your presence shows that a man of the Northern Kingdom can be among my closest nobles, and that my empire is truly one thing. You have been well rewarded for this loyalty, with your lands and your position."

He paused for a moment, then drew his sword.

"But do not, do *not* for one moment think that you are my equal. Do not think that you get to command me, or question me, or change what I decide. If your father is out in the city, he will take his chances with the others there. Do you have any objection, Finnal?"

He saw the other man flinch.

"No, my emperor."

"Good, then I will not have to kill you," Ravin said. He turned to his men. "Now, seal the gates. We will protect this castle and those within. Those without are on their own. They can burn for all I care."

CHAPTER TWENTY EIGHT

When Anders first started creeping toward Devin's home, his plan had been a simple one: grab the sword and kill the pretender to his destiny. Now, with Devin there facing him with the sword in his hand, things were more complex.

"You followed me here," Devin said. The wolf that had been with him in the northern wilds was there by his side now, looking at Anders with far too intelligent eyes.

"I did," Anders admitted, trying to buy a little time in which to think. "Can we talk about this inside?"

"Here is fine," Devin said.

"With people watching?" Anders didn't think that there really would be, or that people would say anything even if they were looking out of their windows at him and the boy who had stolen his destiny. It was simply that, inside, Anders had a better chance of being able to finish this.

"What are you doing here?" Devin asked.

"I told you before," Anders said. "I've come for the sword."

He held out a hand again, hoping against hope that the other boy would simply hand it over. It would make all of this so much more straightforward. It might even mean that Anders didn't need to kill him, because Anders wasn't some cold-blooded murderer. He needed a reason when he killed.

He had one, though. This boy was at the heart of the deception Master Grey had perpetrated on him, had rendered all his sacrifices meaningless just by *existing*. The only reason Anders hadn't killed him already was that he'd needed Devin to finish the blade.

"You want me to just give you my sword?" Devin said. "What *is* this?"

"Master Grey sent me," Anders said, the lie coming smoothly. It wasn't even a lie, not really. Master Grey was the reason he was here, at least.

"You said before that *Lenore* had sent you," Devin said. "You were the one who gave me her message."

"Master Grey came to me afterwards," Anders said. "He sent a kind of ... vision, I guess. He told me about what needed to happen, and he sent me after you."

There was just enough truth in that to make the lie easy. The truth was that Anders had tracked Devin with every step he had taken, cursing the fact that his message had sent him hurrying there before he finished the sword. Once they'd reached the city, he'd waited, giving the other boy time to complete things.

Now, he *would* have the sword. The only question was how.

"Why did he send you?" Devin asked.

"He needs someone who can deliver the sword to where it needs to be," Anders said. "I know he sent you to gather the fragments, but now the sword is needed, and you ... you have your own destiny."

It had been the sense of this boy's destiny that had cost Anders so much, so wouldn't it be poetic to get the sword through it?

Anders heard the wolf growl, low and threatening. This would all have been so much simpler if the creature hadn't been here. Anders had been trained in the arts of stealth as precisely as he had been trained in everything else. Without the creature's sense of smell, he could have gotten into the house, taken the sword, and been gone without even being noticed. Without the boost that came from a conduit like that, Anders could have matched his magic against this boy's easily. Without the additional threat of it beside Devin, he could have stepped forward and simply *taken* the sword.

It might come to that, even now. Anders *would* have the sword, and if he had to fight Devin to get it, then he would. Yet he could see the dangers in doing it. He doubted that Devin had his training with a blade, but he might know enough of what he was doing to be dangerous. He had the wolf to back him up, too.

Anders could *feel* the danger too. The same thing that made the sword so desirable for Anders also made it dangerous to try to take it. He could feel the power within it, the many different strands of magic there together in it, balanced to make the weapon a thing of perfection.

"I ... I'm not sure," Devin said. He held up the sword for Anders to see. "I've put so much work into this. I don't want to just give it away."

Anders couldn't blame him. If the sword were his, he wouldn't let it out of his sight.

"You know that Master Grey makes plans not everyone understands," Anders tried. "We have to trust those plans, and that all the pieces will fit together as they should."

Again, he couldn't help thinking about the irony of that. It had been trusting the sorcerer that had seen so many of his friends killed.

"I know that," Devin said. He frowned and took a step back. "*I* know that, but how do *you*? If the only thing you've seen of Master Grey is an image, how do you know him so well?"

Anders saw him start to back away toward the door of his house.

"And the first time we met, you mentioned the fragments of the sword, but I didn't *tell* Lenore that was what I was going out to find. Who are you really? What are you doing here?"

"You wouldn't believe me if I told you," Anders said, his eyes narrowing in anger. He drew his sword. It had been elegantly made by the finest of smiths, and yet it still seemed like a poor imitation of the sword that Devin held. "You will give me the sword. After everything that you've taken from me, everything that I've suffered ... at least I will get that much out of this."

"After what you've suffered?" Devin said, and of course he sounded confused by that, because Anders was fairly sure that he didn't know any more about Anders than Anders had about him. That didn't make them equals though. "I came back here to find that the woman I love is dead. My parents are gone. Even the sorcerer is missing, so there's no way to find out what's happening with all of this."

For the briefest moment, Anders felt a flicker of pity. After all, he was not cruel, was not evil. He'd spent his whole life trying to live up to the destiny that waited for him, and that called for a hero, not a murderer. Yet the thought of that meant that he was reminded once again of the way Devin had taken everything from him, stepping into the space that should have been Anders's. Anders couldn't forgive that.

"My name is Anders Samis, and I am destined to be the one to wield that sword. Give it to me, or I will take it."

"Try."

Anders struck out with his weapon, moving with all the speed and grace that his lessons had given him. Devin was not as fast, and had to give ground before Anders's attack, but that just meant that his wolf was there, snapping at Anders then dancing out of the way as Anders struck down at it.

Anders circled Devin, shifting guards as he went, looking for an opening. To his surprise, the other boy did a tolerable job of matching the guards that Anders chose, picking ones that closed off the easy angles of attack, making it impossible to simply cut him down in one movement.

That just meant that Anders had to try for a barrage of attacks instead, cutting again and again, trying to get Devin to overcommit to a position so that Anders could take advantage of an opening elsewhere. If the wolf hadn't been there to cover Devin's flank it would have been easy. The other boy was a good enough swordsman, but not a fine one, and Anders had been trained by the best. Anders saw an opening and cut, but Devin brought his blade up to block edge on.

Anders's sword shattered against it. No, it didn't shatter, he realized. Instead, the magic inside Devin's weapon had produced an edge so dangerous it had somehow cut through Anders's sword, leaving him holding only a broken hilt. He threw it at Devin, moving back and trying to think of another option.

He drew up magic, but even as Anders did it, he could feel Devin doing the same. Again, Anders had the feeling that he'd had during their brief interlude of swordplay: that while he was the one with more trained skill, Devin had all the advantages right then. He reached out for that wolf of his, and now his weaving was subtle and complex. It didn't have the formal grace of Anders's attempt, but it was good enough to tangle with it, pulling apart Anders's magic before he could even form it into a coherent attack.

That only increased Anders's fury.

"Look at you!" he shouted, drawing a long knife that he held flat against his forearm. "You aren't me. You could never *be* me. And yet the magus has given you everything. He sent you ahead of me on the quest for the Unfinished Sword, and now you're the one with it, and with a conduit. My friends died, and all the time, he knew that you were ahead anyway, playing his games."

"I don't understand," Devin said. He leveled his sword. "I don't want to kill you, but I will, if I have to."

"Then you'll have to," Anders said. He readied himself to throw himself at Devin. If he could get inside the sweep of the sword in the first rush, that was all that mattered. He would probably be hurt doing it, but if he could kill Devin quickly enough, he might even be able to take control of the conduit. Anders tensed for the leap ...

... and stopped as a shape swooped low over the city, flames pouring from it. Anders saw the dragon, scales blue against the yellow light of its flames in the dark. He knew what it meant, and he felt a rush of horror as the creature set light to a whole swath of the city.

It flew low over the city, and in that moment, Anders knew that there was no more time for his fight with Devin, not when there was a threat there that might kill them all.

Chapter Twenty Nine

As darkness fell Lenore stepped out into the middle of the next village. It would have been so easy to just stay at Lord Carrick's home, to at least rest there, but there was a part of Lenore that would not let her stop like that.

"All of this would still be here in the morning," Odd said. He sat atop a horse because the injury to his leg would not permit him to walk any distance. Lenore had dismounted from hers, because it was important that she could get closer to the people who thronged there, waiting to meet her.

"We have to move quickly," Lenore said. "We're still vulnerable. Until we have enough of an army, Ravin could still strike back and roll over us. Staying moving is our best choice."

That was part of the truth, but the other part was that there were still too many more people who needed to be convinced. Lenore couldn't have sat there in Lord Carrick's castle while that was true.

"I understand," Odd said. He winced slightly. "Although one night in a feather bed would have been pleasant."

"I'm sorry," Lenore said. "Is your wound hurting much?"

"I've had worse," Odd said, as if it was meant to reassure her. It wasn't a *good* thing that this man who had done so much to protect her had been hurt so many times before in his life.

Still, if he was willing to keep going, Lenore was grateful for it. There was an inn here, which called itself the Broken Scale, and Lenore headed for it, letting the crowds of people around her watch her as she went.

That there was an art to being watched by a crowd had been one of the lessons her mother had taught her. Assume that someone is looking every second, maintain your posture, act like the princess you are. Lenore smiled at the thought of those old lessons of her mother's actually being useful for something, then had to hold that smile to keep it from slipping as thoughts of her mother brought back too many memories of the way she'd died.

Lenore could remember more of her mother's words than that, though. *"You have the strength to be a true queen ... People love you, and will listen to you. Now, you have to have the courage to say something."*

They'd been practically the last thing her mother had said to her, and her mother had been right. Lenore was a little shocked by just how much she'd been able to do with her words in the last few days. Now, she needed to keep going.

She waited for Odd to hitch his horse outside the inn, actually helping him down from the saddle before he limped inside with her. The inn was full, in a way that Lenore hadn't expected, yet the people there moved aside so that she could make her way to the bar, where a woman waited, looking at her as if she were some figure out of legend rather than flesh and blood.

She actually curtseyed as Lenore approached. "Your majesty, I'm Yselle. Welcome to my inn. When I heard you were coming ... it was such an honor."

"Stand up, please," Lenore said. "This is your inn and ... wait, *when* did you hear I was coming?"

"People haven't been talking about anything else," Yselle said. "They say you beat Lord Carrick, just you and a mad monk. They say he cut down a hundred men. They say that you stopped them with a word, and that they all threw down their swords and swore to serve you."

"That's ..." Lenore shook her head. Things hadn't happened like that, but she wasn't sure that she could explain it all. Then she realized that she could. "It's not about being special," she said. She looked around at the rest of them there, and raised her voice. "You all think that I'm something unstoppable, something that will sweep away Ravin like he's nothing."

Lenore leaned against the bar for support, but she made sure that she stood tall and straight. Let them see the queen that she could become, that she *was*.

"The truth, though, is that I'm just a person," Lenore said. "I listened to a lot of stories as a child; stories of perfect princesses and noble warriors who could take on any number of foes without being hurt. But you, all of you, know that life isn't like that. Odd, how many men did you kill at Lord Carrick's castle."

The knight stood there among the people, a faint look of concentration on his face. "Perhaps half a dozen."

"And he was wounded doing that," Lenore said. "I have no special power to overcome Ravin and his men just because I am a princess."

She paused for a moment, letting that sink in. Lenore could hear a few of them muttering. This clearly wasn't the speech that they had been expecting to hear. She kept going.

"You do, though," she said. "All of you, working together. It is easy to sit back and wait for someone else to solve things, because someone else is special, someone else has the power to do it. Yet the only way that we succeed in this is if you are prepared to take the step that matters. Stand with me, and we can take back this kingdom. Stand with me, and—"

Lenore saw the man advancing through the crowd toward her, but for a second or two her mind didn't register it as anything important. He was just a man trying to get closer, to listen better, an ordinary-looking man with medium-brown hair and a bland, forgettable expression.

It was only as he got closer that Lenore saw the flash of the knife in his hand.

"Odd!" Lenore said, trying to draw the knight's attention to the man, but it seemed that Odd's eyes were already on him.

Unfortunately, the knifeman was already in motion.

"Death to traitors!" he shouted, and lunged forward for Lenore, his knife sweeping toward her throat. On another day, perhaps Odd would have intercepted that blow, as he had intercepted others aimed at ending her life. Now though, Lenore saw him move slowly, hindered by his injured leg, drawing his sword quick enough but not able to cross that distance.

Lenore had only a fraction of a second to decide what to do. She had no room to dodge back, and in any case that would open up her throat to his attack, so she ducked her head and threw herself forward instead, hoping that at least she could avoid a fatal slash.

She felt pain flare across her cheek as the slashing knife bit into it, and now she was falling, tumbling to the ground while around her people screamed in terror. She stared up at her attacker, who was already kneeling to try to finish the job with thrusts. Lenore grabbed out for his knife arm, but it only meant that he slashed another cut across the back of her forearm, making her cry out.

Then Odd was there. His injury might have bought the attacker a second in which to strike, but now Odd's blade was out, and he struck even as Lenore's attacker raised his arm for another blow. Odd's cut took his hand off at the wrist in a gout of blood. Lenore saw him reverse the direction of the blade, and now it sliced through flesh and bone as it slammed into the would-be assassin's neck, taking his head from his shoulders in one smooth movement.

He collapsed atop Lenore, and for a moment, the horror of it was too much. Around her, people were screaming, and there was blood everywhere, the chaos of it too great to keep track of. A part of Lenore wanted to just lie there until all of this went away, but she knew that she couldn't. She pushed herself back to her feet. She needed people to see that she was still alive, since presumably the point of sending an assassin here like this had been to make sure that everyone saw that she was dead.

Around her, she could see people pushing and shoving, some trying to get closer to see what was happening. Odd appeared to be holding those back, leaning on the bar with his sword held in both hands as he looked out for other potential assassins. Lenore could see the potential for all of this to go wrong, and for people to get hurt, the longer this went on.

"Stop!" she called out over the chaos, and the force of it was enough that people *did* stop, turning to look at her.

"Lenore, stay back," Odd said. "You're hurt."

"Do you think I didn't know that this could happen?" Lenore said.

Her cheek burned like fire, and very deliberately, she put her hand to it, so that it came away wet with blood. She held it up so that the others could see it. "Do you think I believed I could get through this without bleeding?"

She looked around them levelly, waiting very deliberately, letting them see her hurt but not dead, still standing in spite of the injuries that had been inflicted on her.

"I am not some meek, weak princess," she said. "I am not going to wilt and run away just because I have been hurt. The girl I was would be terrified right now that her face would scar. Now, I'm more frightened of what is happening to the people of my kingdom, of the people who are dying or enslaved in Royalsport while the worst that has happened to me is a little blood."

She stepped out among them. There was a danger to that, because there might be more assassins, but right then, Lenore didn't care.

"I will be hurt again before this is done," she said. "Perhaps I will even die. It doesn't matter. I will give my blood a hundred times over if it will save the people of this kingdom, *my* kingdom. The question is, will you?"

The cheer that started around Lenore shook the inn to its rafters. She knew in that moment that she would have all the people she needed. They would follow her, and they would die for her if necessary, the same way that she was prepared to die for her kingdom.

Chapter Thirty

Aurelle felt grubby as she started to make her way back toward the House of Sighs. Not that she'd had to do anything, particularly. It was just that now, even the thought of pretending to work for Finnal and his father again was hard to stomach.

She strolled down through the city as darkness fell, glancing back occasionally to make sure that there were no Quiet Men following her. As she did so, Aurelle told herself again and again that she was doing the right thing, and that she'd done more good already with a couple of subtle hints than outright murder ever could have.

Even so, it was hard to believe. She found herself thinking of Greave, and how much she'd lost when he died. She wanted revenge for his death. She wanted Finnal and Duke Viris dead for what they'd done to him, and for the person they'd made her be.

Aurelle could imagine Greave's response to that, of course. He would want her to put it to one side, would want her to be a better person. He wasn't here to tell her that, though, so the most Aurelle could do was try to remind herself that at least this way, she had a chance of bringing down the whole of the invasion, as well as just the men she wanted dead.

She kept making her way on through the city, taking a winding route that would allow her to be sure that there was no trouble coming. Aurelle was confident that she could deal with anyone who tried to follow her, but she could do it more easily, and more subtly, if she saw it coming early. Spot an opponent early enough, and she could simply lose them in the city as she headed back to the House of Sighs.

It wouldn't have mattered how little attention she was paying though, when it came to the moment the fight started in the noble quarter. The magic and the explosions rocked the streets around her, lighting up the sky with their energy. For a moment, Aurelle could only stand and stare, trying to make some kind of sense of it all.

Then the bulk of a huge, scaled creature swooped in over the city, flames pouring from its mouth. Aurelle heard the whoomph of rooftops igniting, saw the night give way to light as the flames brightened it, and as the magic thrown back at the creature burst around it.

For a moment, Aurelle could only stand there, staring at it, her mind refusing to supply a name for something so big, so terrifying, so impossible. Then it did, and it was like the word "dragon" snapped something in her. She turned and started to run.

Even as she did so, Aurelle dared a glance back. She saw the dragon wheel this way and that, pouring fire down seemingly indiscriminately. Almost inevitably, she saw it swing her way, and a line of fire burned its way along the street in her wake.

Aurelle ran, blindly and filled with terror, taking twists and turns at random. Flames burst around her, and for a moment, she thought that the creature must be targeting her. That thought awakened a kind of fear in her that was so old she didn't even have a name for it, something primal and shiver inducing in the knowledge that something more powerful than her wanted her dead.

Then the dragon swooped past, turning a house in front of Aurelle into a blazing candle, and kept going. This wasn't about her, it wasn't hunting her, and there should have been some measure of relief in that, but faced with the destruction it was wreaking, Aurelle couldn't feel anything except the need to get away.

Aurelle kept making her way through the city, reasoning that she had more hope of surviving if she made it back to the stone and slate of the House of Sighs, rather than risking being caught out on the street. She could still see the dragon, the moonlight and the light of its own flames making it easy to pick out. Even as she watched, it hovered in place, spitting fire down toward the city below.

It was hard to make any sense of it. There didn't seem to be any pattern or point to the dragon's attacks. Instead, it seemed to be zigzagging its way across the city, burning things below seemingly at random, tearing off roofs and smashing aside walls. It reminded Aurelle a little of a hound searching for its prey, but without the ability to smell it. Was that it? Had its brief battle with whoever was using magic in the noble district blinded it to whatever it was looking for? Was it flailing blindly now?

Aurelle knew she didn't have time for questions like that, because at any moment the dragon could swoop around again. There were already flames everywhere she looked, black smoke billowing into the streets. Around Aurelle, those who could manage it started to try to form bucket chains down to the rivers, trying to fight the worst of the fires even while they had no hope of fighting the dragon.

Aurelle kept running. She made it down to the river, and to one of the partially rebuilt bridges, the span of it bridged with planks in place of its usual stones. There was a guard there, but he was so busy staring up at the night sky that he had no hope of stopping Aurelle. By the time he started to shout a challenge, she was already past him, sprinting across the planks of the bridge, heading on into the entertainment district.

Still, fire rained down on the city. Aurelle had been there in Astare when Greave had burned the docks. She had set light to its library herself, to give them a chance to get away. None of those flames even began to compare to the ones that ate at some of the buildings around Aurelle. She heard the whoosh of flame somewhere behind her, and threw herself flat to the cobbles as fire flashed past her, setting light to a fruit seller's stall. It all but exploded with the heat of the flames, fragments of wood flying past her.

Aurelle got up, because to stay where she was meant death. She made it to her hands and knees, forced her way to her feet, and kept running. Above her, the dragon struck out at the surrounding buildings with more than flames now, striking out with its tail and claws. The sheer power of it was enough to send stones flying, lumps of rock the size of Aurelle's head hammering into the ground around her.

Aurelle dodged her way between the falling stones like some dainty noblewoman trying to pick her way through the rain, except that *this* rain would kill her if it touched her, the stones smashing into shrapnel as they struck the cobblestones.

She could do this, *would* do this. She had been trained to survive the worst things that might happen, had already survived the chaos of an invasion. If she kept moving, and used the most solid-looking buildings for cover, she might be able to avoid the flames well enough. As for the dragon's impact on the walls around it ... all Aurelle could do was wait and hope.

Briefly, the dragon's efforts turned in another direction, striking at a different part of the city, and Aurelle saw her chance. If she ran now, she had a good chance to make it to the House of Sighs. At the very least, she could get to the next safe spot, judge her next run, working her way forward little by little.

She broke from her cover, and ran for all she was worth, hurrying along back alleys, leaping over a small fence and keeping going. She was still running when she saw the girl.

She couldn't have been more than around five or six. She was tiny and soot smudged, looking around with the blank expression of someone who couldn't take in the horror of everything that was happening to her. The terror-filled part of Aurelle wanted to keep running, not stopping until she got to safety.

She *did* stop, though, reaching out a hand toward the girl.

"What are you doing out here?" she asked.

For a moment, the girl seemed too terrified to answer, but then she managed a couple of words, pointing.

"My mother ..."

Aurelle followed the line of her pointing finger. She saw a charred shape there, among a section of blackened stones. Aurelle made a decision in that moment, reaching out and taking hold of the girl, lifting her smoothly.

"We're going to get you somewhere safe," she said. "Come on."

She ran with the girl, heading in the direction of the House of Sighs. The bulk of it was there ahead. Just a little longer, and they'd be there. She'd wasted too much time by stopping, and the additional weight of the girl was slowing her down. One glance behind showed her that the dragon was closing in again, heading back in their direction. As short as the distance was to the House of Sighs, Aurelle knew that they would never make it in time.

She looked around at the surrounding buildings, trying to work out which would offer the most safety, yet they all looked so very fragile in comparison to the House. Swallowing, Aurelle realized what she had to do, making the kind of decision that she'd always known that she would have to make one day. That didn't make it any easier. She didn't want to die, but looking down at the child she held, she knew that she wanted this girl to die even less.

"When I say," she said, setting the girl down, "I want you to run to that building and bang on the door. Don't stop, and don't look back. Tell them that Aurelle sent you and that they're to keep you safe."

She watched the dragon closing in, then pushed the girl in the direction of the House of Sighs.

"Run!" she yelled and the child set off. Even as she did, Aurelle was already standing there, waving, making as big of a target of herself as possible. She darted off in the opposite direction, back among the houses. The dragon followed, and Aurelle felt the briefest flash of relief that it was following her, not the girl, but then the terror was back, propelling her forward.

The dragon was almost overhead, and Aurelle dove into one of the small buildings to the side. She paused there for a moment, looking up and trying to listen, attempting to guess where the dragon was by sound alone. She heard, and felt, the house shake as something struck it. Aurelle started to run for the door, knowing that this was only temporary safety at best. A second impact came above her.

She ran harder, but it still wasn't fast enough. A third impact came, and now stones were falling around her. The last thought Aurelle had was that she hoped the girl had made it to the House of Sighs, and then something struck her, consuming her in darkness.

CHAPTER THIRTY ONE

Devin stood there, waiting for Anders to fling himself at him, as Devin knew that he must. Devin didn't want him to, didn't want to strike out with Loss and kill him, but he could see the moments that would follow as clearly as if players were acting them out for him to watch. Anders would grab for a knife and attack, hoping that speed would be enough to overcome him. Devin would cut back, and the sword would bite deep ...

Devin wasn't sure what to feel about that, even though Sigil seemed to be growling in anticipation of the moment by Devin's side. He hated the thought of killing someone he didn't even know. Yet Anders had been quick enough to strike at *him*, and if he came at Devin again, Devin wouldn't hesitate. He wouldn't have a choice.

Inexplicably, Devin saw Anders take a step back, staring at something in the sky. Devin heard him gasp, and yet for a moment, Devin didn't dare look round. Then Anders's eyes widened.

"Down!" he yelled, and the urgency of it was enough that Devin threw himself flat, even as Anders did.

Flames roared overhead, burning the ground somewhere beyond Devin. He saw a wooden house go up in flames, the heat of it instant and total. Devin saw the shape that passed over, its bulk huge and terrifying, the blue of its scales glowing with reflected flames. That blue was familiar, and Devin found himself thinking about the dragon he'd met in the forest. This seemed so much bigger; it couldn't be the same one, could it?

That familiarity did nothing to wash away the fear of it as it lashed out at the city almost indiscriminately, burning at random, plunging down at roofs to strike with claws and tail. It flew back into the city, attacking something else, more flames coming as Devin struggled back to his feet. Across from him, Anders was doing the same.

"Thank you," Devin said.

"I wasn't saving you," Anders said. "I was protecting the sword."

Even so, Devin was grateful, because the other boy had probably saved his life.

"I hope that you're better prepared than you seem," Anders said. "Come on."

He started off toward the city.

"You think I'm going to follow you?" Devin shouted after him.

Anders stopped and pointed at the dragon. "*That* means that it's time to start actually doing the things we're destined to do."

"*What* things?" Devin demanded. "The only part Master Grey told me about was forging the sword."

Anders's expression was contemptuous. "The old fool really told you nothing, didn't he? We fight the dragon. We stop it. What else do you think the sword is for?"

He didn't wait any longer, but set off into the city. Devin stared down at Sigil, as if the wolf might have some kind of answers for him.

"What do you think?" he asked the wolf. "Should we follow?"

He wasn't about to trust Anders so soon after the other boy had been trying to kill him, but at the same time, he could *see* the dragon ahead in the city, and could see what needed to be done. He reached out for Sigil's fur, the increased connection to magic letting him see the dragon in a new way. Magic curled around it, and when it breathed flame, Devin could see the power in that flame, the instinctive manipulation of the magic of the world that produced it.

If anyone could stop something like that, wasn't it someone with training in magic, and a weapon filled with it? Put like that, it didn't matter whether this was Anders's idea or not. What mattered was that Devin could help, and so he needed to.

He rushed into the city, in the direction that the dragon had flown, and in which Anders had run. Sigil loped by his side, and Devin could feel the power of Loss thrumming in his hand. He picked a way through the destruction on the streets, through the fires and the partially collapsed buildings, keeping his eyes on the bulk of the dragon above.

"There!" Anders called, pointing to a tall, flat-roofed building. "If it's trying to pick apart buildings, we'll meet it there."

He led the way to the door and kicked it open in one smooth movement. A woman cried out as they pushed their way into the house, but Devin was already climbing, heading up toward that roof. He, Anders, and Sigil hurried toward the roof, making their way up flight after flight of stairs until they came up onto it, under the stars.

The dragon was still causing destruction around them, sending bursts of flame down onto the streets, so that fire rose in response. It tore another roof away, peering inside the way that Devin might have looked into a box.

"It's searching for something," Devin said. "How do we get its attention?"

"Like this," Anders said, and Devin felt him send a burst of magic in the direction of the creature, as quickly and easily as Devin might have taken a step.

He saw the dragon rear back as if someone had struck it, and take to the air again, heading straight for them. Devin felt fear rising inside him, but he held steady, taking Loss in both hands and forcing himself to hold his position as it came at them.

The first gout of flame that it spat out struck the building lower down, and Devin felt the impact of it as a shudder in the building. A second such shudder came as the dragon landed on the flat surface of the roof, wings spread for balance, great head moving back and forth as it stared at them.

Devin readied himself to strike, trying to work out the best spot to plunge Loss into, and it seemed almost like the dragon was staring at him in the same way, great, catlike eyes sweeping over him as if trying to work out which part to eat first.

"What are you waiting for?" Anders asked. "Kill it!"

Yet the more Devin stared at the dragon, the more certain he was that this was the same one he had met out in the forest. The blue scales were the same shade, and the eyes had the same depth of intelligence to them. He'd met this dragon before, and it had let him live then.

In that moment, Devin didn't want to fight it. He didn't want to kill it, in spite of the destruction that raged around the city. He lowered his blade.

"I'm not going to hurt you," he said, hoping that the dragon could understand him. "And I don't think you want to hurt me either."

"What are you doing?" Anders demanded. "It's a dragon. You have a sword that will kill it. End this."

The dragon loomed over them, and for a moment Devin thought that he'd misjudged this. He was sure that he was going to die in that moment, burned or crushed between those jaws.

Then the dragon turned away and leapt from the building, powerful wings taking it out into the dark to continue its search.

"What are you doing?" Anders shouted. "You had it there, where you wanted it. You could have killed it!"

"It wasn't..." How could Devin explain this to the other boy? More to the point, why should he? "I'm not just going to kill something because you say I should. Not that long ago, you were trying to kill me."

"And I wish I'd succeeded," Anders said. "At least then, *I'd* have had the sword to kill that thing. Why would the sorcerer pick a *coward* for this?"

Devin ignored him. He was too busy looking over the roof at the dragon as it continued its trail of devastation. As he looked down though, his eyes fell on the side of the building, and the flames there. His nose started to fill with the scent of smoke rising from it, as the fire started by the dragon's breath started to grow.

"We need to get out of here," Anders said. "I'm not burning to death because you failed to kill a dragon."

He started to lead the way down through the house, and Devin followed, Sigil loping on ahead. Around him, the inhabitants of the house were rushing to get free, and Devin saw Anders ushering them out with obvious care and concern. Somehow, it was worse that this young man who'd tried to kill him was also a good person who would make sure that a whole family would get out of a burning house. Flames licked at the wooden frame, and the smoke was thick and acrid enough that Devin had to hold his sleeve over his mouth to try to block it.

A cry came from back up the stairs.

"Ana!" a woman said.

Devin frowned at that. "Who's Ana?"

"My daughter," she said. "I thought that she'd gotten out already."

Devin cursed, then looked back. "I'll go. The rest of you get out while you can. Sigil, go with them."

"Here," Anders said. "Take my cloak."

He tossed Devin a dark cloak, lined with fur. Devin took it gratefully. He hurried back up the stairs, and since the wolf didn't follow, Devin guessed that he understood the danger. Devin ran up to a room on the floor above where cries for help were coming. There were flames around the doorway, and Devin was grateful for Anders's cloak in that moment, because it meant that he could wrap it around himself, plunging through the flames of the doorway and into the room beyond.

There was a girl there, looking terrified of the flames, backing away from the door. Devin held out a hand to her. "Ana? It's all right. I'm going to get you out of here."

Even as he said it, the lintel of the door gave way, half collapsing across the doorway, flames growing up around it. They wouldn't be getting out that way now. Devin saw a window across the other side of the room.

"We'll have to go out the window," he said. Taking Loss, he smashed the window, creating an opening that they could get through. He tossed the sword down, because he didn't want to risk landing on it. "Come on, I'll lower you down."

"I can't do it," the girl said.

"You can," Devin assured her. "You have to."

He helped the girl through, holding onto her arms so that he could get her closer to the floor. "Roll when you hit the ground."

He let go, watching her drop. She hit the ground and rolled as Devin had told her. Devin breathed a sigh of relief when she came up to her feet again.

Now it was his turn, and there were no helping hands to lower him closer to the ground. All he could do was climb out, and then jump.

For a moment, he hung in the air, then the ground came up to meet him, far too quickly. It smashed the air from his lungs as he struck it, and for a moment, his head swam.

When he managed to stand, the family were there, standing around him. Devin was happy to see them all safe, Sigil standing among them. He reached around for the sword.

Devin froze in horror. He couldn't find it. If it weren't for one other thing, he might have thought it was nothing, that it had merely fallen into a spot where he couldn't see it. There was a face missing from the group, though.

Anders was gone, as well as the sword. He'd taken it, and now he was gone.

CHAPTER THIRTY TWO

When the dragon started to attack, Renard ran toward the walls of the castle. Right then, they seemed like the only place of safety in the city. At the very least, they were nonflammable in a way that so much of the city wasn't. For Renard, an inability to burn was making its way close to the top of the list of things he looked for in a hiding place right then.

The fact that the sorcerer's apparatus lay waiting in his tower, able to contain the power of the amulet, only made it more promising. He got closer, and an arrow slammed into the ground in front of him.

"No one comes in!" a voice called.

"But there's a *dragon* chasing me," Renard said.

"Then find somewhere to hide. No one enters, by order of the emperor. Now go, before the next arrow's in your heart."

Renard wanted to argue with that, but he'd always found that in such arguments, the people with all the weaponry tended to win. Besides, he had bigger problems, in the form of the dragon still wheeling here and there over the city, striking seemingly at random. The fact that it was doing that and not chasing Renard directly suggested that Master Grey's spell to hide the amulet was working.

Now, he just had to get to some kind of safety. He headed back in the direction of the noble quarter's houses, hoping that he could find somewhere to hide among them. It meant going back close to where Master Grey was still fighting with the Hidden, and now it seemed that he was giving ground, throwing attacks but yielding after each one, as if knowing that he couldn't take on all three at once.

Renard gave them a wide berth, heading around them, but now there was another problem. Renard felt the moment that Master Grey's spell snapped, the slow drain from the amulet seeming to flicker and shift slightly.

If that wasn't enough of a clue, the dragon swung back toward him, moving too fast to hope to outrun, its mouth open wide for the burst of flame that Renard was sure would kill him.

Of course, Renard ran anyway. A death that he could put off for another minute was definitely better than facing up to one right now. He darted left and right, knowing instinctively that straight lines would be a bad idea. A jet of flame shot past him as he dodged, and Renard kept running.

The dragon swooped past him now, turning in the air and hovering on great blue wings the way a kestrel might have while it stared at him, great yellow eyes regarding him as nothing more than prey.

"Here," Renard said. He took out the amulet. "If *this* is why you're chasing me, take it. Do you think I want to be chased across the kingdom by dragons? Just calm down."

He held the amulet up, ready to toss away from himself while he ran in the other direction. As a thief, he objected on principle to having to simply abandon something he'd worked so hard for, but on the other hand he objected to being burned alive even more. He tensed himself for the throw.

To his surprise, the dragon gave up on its roaring and flames. It landed before Renard, looking at him quizzically. Renard felt…

…*the need to be close to the amulet. The presence of the human. The words that Alith had not been able to ignore, to be calm …*

Renard came back to himself with a start, breathing hard, barely able to believe this, in spite of everything that had happened to him recently. Even compared to the Hidden and the dragons and the rest, *this* seemed impossible. He could still feel a kind of connection to the dragon in front of him, the amulet seeming to provide a kind of… conduit; that was the best word for it. He was connected to this dragon somehow through it.

Renard thought back. He'd felt this before, felt it even back in the temple where he'd gotten the amulet.

The only question was just how much that connection could do. The urge to find out overcame even his fear then. He wanted to know, and if it might save his life, that was even better.

"Spread your wings," Renard said. When the dragon did exactly that, he could barely contain his gasp of disbelief. Knowing that the amulet was powerful and seeing it with his own eyes were two different things. "Close them." Again, it obeyed.

The amulet let him control the dragon. The reality of that was still taking time to sink in. After all the strange things that Renard had seen, it was still a lot. Actual control of a dragon?

Renard suspected that it wasn't quite as simple as that, because when was anything in his life as simple as that? In any case, he could feel the effort and the concentration that it took in order to make this work.

Still, he had to try.

"Come with me," he said, turning in the direction of the spot where Master Grey was fighting with the Hidden. It seemed so obvious to use the dragon to help, and Renard would have done exactly that except for one of those small inconveniences that seemed to litter his life:

There was no sign of Master Grey now, only the Hidden stalking toward him. Thanks to the masks it was impossible to guess at their expressions, but Renard could feel the hatred coming off them perfectly well.

"The amulet," Void said as he stepped forward.

Wrath was there, hands already working in the gestures of a spell. Beside him, Verdant seemed to be calling up vines, ready to strike. Renard stared at them, and he found that he'd had enough of running, enough of hiding. Of course, the fact that he had a dragon backing him up probably had something to do with that, but he didn't feel that it ruined the effect.

"Kill them," Renard whispered, pushing the need for it through the link between him and the dragon. He concentrated, and the dragon roared in response.

It surged forward, the ground shaking as its clawed feet struck down. It went straight at the Hidden, flames bursting out toward them, white hot and deadly. Wrath managed to block those, throwing up what looked like a shield of rock and flames that absorbed the impact, standing with his legs braced, pushing back against the fire even as the dragon kept coming forward.

Verdant threw vines around the creature's legs, and it snapped them. Void tried something that seemed to involve planes of darkness pressing in with sharp edges, but the dragon battered them aside too, Renard's will holding it to its course, forcing it forward even though it bellowed as Void tried some new magic. Wrath seemed to be preparing for some greater attack...

That was when the dragon reached him, its sinuous neck snaking down so that its jaws could clamp down on the big man's torso. They closed with the agonizing crack of bones breaking, and Wrath screamed. The dragon continued to bite down, and now those teeth managed to shear all the way through the member of the Hidden so that his legs and torso fell separately to the ground as he died. The power within him seemed to come up in a rush, consuming him in a fire so hot that it hurt the eyes to look upon.

"Withdraw," Void said, and Verdant didn't hesitate. In just a second, the two were finding ways to escape, Void stepping into a shadow and disappearing, Verdant being borne away a wave of living plants.

"How do you like *that*?" Renard called after them. It was a mistake. The moment he took to celebrate was all it took for his tenuous grip on the dragon to break, his concentration giving way as the effort involved became too much. The dragon roared in its freedom and shot fire into the air. It spun around quickly, and too late, Renard realized that he was standing in the wrong spot. Even then, if he hadn't just put so much into controlling the dragon he might have managed to dodge it, but now there was no time.

The tail struck him squarely in the ribs, sending him flying toward the outer wall of a nearby noble house. Renard struck it with a thud that he felt through his whole body, and blinding lights seemed to flash in front of him as his head hit the stone. He felt the amulet slide from his hand. The dragon turned to him again, and now its claws slammed into the building, sending stones tumbling down on top of Renard. It was all he could do to get his arms up to shield his head from the worst of it.

Somewhere in it, he must have blacked out. When he came to, Renard could feel the pressure of the rocks on him, see the darkness surrounding him. He pushed his way up out of the rubble, slowly and carefully, pushing aside rocks until he came out into the open air.

In the distance, he could just about make out the form of the dragon. It was flying away through the night sky, bursts of flame occasionally illuminating it as it went. Renard breathed a sigh of relief that it was finally gone.

The others were gone too. There was no sign of the remaining Hidden, but also no sign of Master Grey. Had he gone ahead to his tower or retreated from Royalsport completely? There seemed to be no way for Renard to know.

Every part of him ached, but even so he took the time to start lifting aside stones, looking for the amulet. It had to be here somewhere.

He was still searching when he saw a girl limping away from the castle, carrying what looked like the broken head of a spear and staggering every few paces. She was shorter than Renard and slenderly built, yet there was a sense of toughness to her that came through even though she looked as though she'd been beaten half to death. Behind her, the doors to the castle were starting to open again now that the dragon was gone, and soldiers were coming out, heading in the direction of the girl.

Renard knew that he should ignore her. He needed to concentrate on getting the amulet. Yet it was safe enough wherever it was under the rubble. Even if soldiers found it, they wouldn't be able to touch it safely, while this girl clearly wasn't going to be able to limp away fast enough on her own.

Renard hesitated, but he'd always had an affinity for people running away from soldiers, largely because they'd so often been him. He hurried over to her, and stopped short as she brought the spear head up, the tip of it quivering just a little way from his face.

"I'm not here to hurt you," Renard said. "I'm here to help."

"I don't want…" she began, but almost fell against Renard. He caught her, holding her up.

"You'll never make it alone," Renard said. "And I've no reason to love guardsmen. Come on, I know somewhere safe."

Well, safe-ish. It would probably be safe enough for the girl, but with the way things had gone, Meredith was probably going to kill him. This did *not* count as keeping out of trouble.

"All right," the girl said, and together they started to limp out into the night. Renard just hoped that they could do it fast enough to avoid the soldiers.

CHAPTER THIRTY THREE

O dd could only stare in admiration as Lenore led her army back toward the farm. The first rays of dawn were breaking over the horizon, illuminating her as she rode. He felt a hint of guilt as he saw the cut across her cheek, carefully stitched back at the inn, but that guilt gave way to pride at the way she rode without giving any hint of pain.

His own pain was troubling him, but only because of the way it had slowed him down back at the inn. With all that was coming, he needed to be healthy, able to fight at his best. At least when they got back, Erin would be able to take over guarding her sister. Maybe Odd would talk to her again, and try to mend some of the divisions that had come between them.

The windmill over the farm stood up ahead, so that Odd could make out the slow turn of its blades, the lower shape of the farmhouse beside it.

"Almost there," he said to Lenore. "We'll be able to get some rest there."

She managed a smile in response. "We'll have little time for that. This is just a beginning, Odd. We still need so many more people for a true army, and we need to train them."

"Erin will have been working hard with those there," Odd said. "We can do this, but not all in one go. Don't push yourself too hard, my queen."

"The kingdom is relying on me," Lenore said.

"And that is why we must make sure that we will do this in a way that will succeed," Odd said. "We will train your people, plan what must be done, and rest."

"It would be good to get some sleep," Lenore said.

Around them, the people who had followed them from the inn were also looking tired. They'd walked and ridden through the night to be here, both ordinary people and Lord Carrick's former troops. Odd was sure that some had slipped off into the dark at different points, although not as many as he might have expected. Lenore's presence held them together in a way that most things would not have.

They got closer to the farm now, and in the growing light, Odd saw something impossible.

"Odd..." Lenore said.

"I see them," Odd said. There were people encamped there, far more than Odd would ever have expected. He saw the banners of several minor noble houses there, but also plenty of ordinary-looking people. He found himself thinking of the people who had slipped off in the night. What if they'd been going to tell others? And what about the way they'd already heard of Lenore at the inn? What about the assassin who had been waiting for Lenore?

In that moment, Odd started to realize the scale of this. The news of what Lenore was doing was spreading like wildfire, and it was bringing in people from all around the kingdom.

"How many are there?" Lenore asked.

Odd had some experience judging the size of armies. He knew how to count campfires, and to guess at the number of men around them. It was harder when the forces weren't well ordered though, and on the route in, it was impossible to see all of them.

"I'm not sure," he said. "Thousands."

He saw Lenore kick her horse forward, and he dug his heels into the horse's flanks to keep up. As they approached, there were men waiting there on guard, as there should be in a well-ordered camp, and a shout went up from somewhere up near the top of the windmill, where a sentry would be able to see for leagues around.

He saw Harris and Tess come out from their farm to meet them, and Odd was grateful for Harris's hand holding his bridle, steading the horse while Odd dismounted. It meant he could do it without putting weight on his injured leg.

"We're so glad you're back," Tess said. "People have been coming here from *everywhere*. There have been lords trying to tell us that they should have our rooms."

"I hope you didn't give them up," Lenore said.

Harris shook his head. "I wasn't about to stand for that."

"I imagine Erin wouldn't either," Odd added. That earned him a worried look.

"She ... she hasn't been here," Harris the miller said.

"What?" Lenore said. "What happened?"

"She left shortly after you did," Tess explained. "We don't know where she went."

Odd knew, or at least he could guess, and he could see that Lenore could guess as well, because he could see the blood draining from her face in a look of horror.

"She's gone to do it, hasn't she?" Lenore said. "She's gone to try to kill him."

Odd could only nod in response to that. It was like the time she'd killed the assassins in Lenore's chambers, all over again. Erin always had to do things her own way, driven by her own anger. She couldn't stick to a plan.

Odd would have been amused by how close that sounded to his former self, if he wasn't all too aware of how much damage that version of him had done.

"I'll go fetch her back," he said. "I'll get her safe here before she does anything stupid."

Lenore looked like she was about to agree, but then, to Odd's surprise, she shook her head.

"No, there's nothing you can do," Lenore said. "She's already gone, and even if you catch up to her, do you really think that you'd be able to persuade her to come back?"

"I ... no," Odd admitted. "Not after everything that's happened."

"I love my sister," Lenore said, "and I want her safe. I hate the idea of her being out there alone and in danger." Odd heard her sigh. "But I want everyone else safe too, and that means winning this war. I need you with me to do that, Odd. I need the skills and the knowledge you have. My sister ... Erin has the skills to keep herself safe."

She didn't look happy about it, but Odd could understand the decision. Lenore was a queen now, fighting for her country. She had to act like a queen, and that meant that she couldn't just follow her heart and go after her sister.

"I need to go and meet with the people here," Lenore said. "You should get some rest, Odd."

Odd knew that she was being kind, but if she had the strength to be a queen, he would find the strength to be everything that he had sworn to be. "I will come with you."

He followed her, out among the campfires and the tents. With every step that Lenore took, men looked at her with awe, or bowed, or called out their loyalty.

"We came as soon as we heard, your majesty!" a man called out.

"They say you threw down Lord Carrick. Anyone who'll overthrow an evil lord like that has my support!"

"We'll fight to the death for you!"

There were so many of them, and Odd could make out the different groups among them. He saw the bandits who had tried to rob them, and one of them actually waved a salute in his direction. He saw peasant folks armed with agricultural tools and simple weapons, many with the kinds of bows they might have used for hunting or poaching. He saw foot soldiers with spears or axes, armored in mail. He saw a few more heavily armored figures, nobles and their retinues, swords and horses well cared for. He and Lenore made their way through all of them, to their heart.

There seemed to be an argument going on there. Three men in rich velvet and adorned with jewelry stood beneath three banners, each one showing signs of his anger. One thin-faced man of advancing years was pale, his expression drawn. A bigger, bulkier man had gone red in the face . A slightly younger man dressed for battle was waving his arms wildly.

"... And I say that it's not *about* the order of precedence, or the number of men you've brought," the young man was saying.

"How can you say that?" the older man said. "If precedence means nothing, what are we fighting for?"

"We're fighting for the kingdom," the big man said. "And I have brought the most men to support that cause."

"What is this argument about?" Lenore asked, so calmly that it cut through the arguing smoothly. The men looked to her, and offered her bows so deep that they almost made Odd laugh.

"Your majesty," the older man said. "I am Lord Renslip, and these are—"

"Lord Welles and Lord Ness," Lenore finished for him, pointing to the bigger one and the younger one respectively. "I know who you are, my lords. I'm asking what your argument is about."

"We were merely debating who would be most suited to aid you in commanding your armies in the field," Lord Welles said. "Obviously, you are our queen, but we will also need a leader on the ground who has the skills and training for battle."

"And you thought that you would decide it among yourselves?" Lenore asked. Odd was impressed by the calm way in which she said that, while still managing to put enough disapproval into it that the three men backed away instantly.

"I appreciate your presence, my lords," Lenore said. "We will not win back this kingdom without the help of everyone here, but I want to be clear about one thing: I am queen. I will ask for advice, but I will not have my decisions made for me."

As in so many moments like this, people seemed to react to her words in a way that they never would have if Odd had said them. It was just one of the things that made her such an impressive leader.

"Forgive us, my queen," Lord Ness said. "We meant only—"

"You meant to establish your positions in the new order," Lenore said. "But in doing so, your arguing could have torn my armies apart. *My* armies." She gestured to all the men waiting around them. "If she had still been here, I would have given my sister command. She was a Knight of the Spur, and noble enough for any of you, and had fought in the battle for Royalsport. I take it those qualifications would have been acceptable to you all?"

Odd saw them all nod quickly, even though they would probably have argued if Erin had actually been there.

"Then it is just as well that we have another with such qualifications," Lenore said, and Odd realized what she intended, even as she looked at him. "Odd, you will command in battle."

"Me?" Odd said. He started to shake his head.

"It's what I want," Lenore said. "You have no ties to any one noble house, and the ordinary soldiers will respect you. More importantly, I trust you. You will command, and any man who tries to gainsay that will answer to me."

There was determination there that made it impossible for Odd to argue. He bowed. "Yes, your majesty."

"Then prepare my armies, General Odd. We will rest today, but tomorrow ... tomorrow we will march to Royalsport."

CHAPTER THIRTY FOUR

A s the first rays of dawn touched Nerra's face, she sat atop one of Astare's walls, watching the city being torn apart, and all she could think of was how her brother wouldn't have been able to watch any of it.

This is necessary, Shadr said. *We must be protected.*

Nerra understood that, but there was still something sad about watching the Lesser plunge into the depths of Astare's great library, about them tearing out possessions from homes and throwing papers into the air as they searched. It was like watching an army sack the city, but with all the fury that the howling fury of the Lesser brought with them.

"Is this what it will be like when we take the rest of the kingdom?" Nerra asked. "This much destruction?"

Sometimes destruction is necessary, but no, Shadr said. *We come to conquer, not to destroy utterly. Human things will serve, as they should.*

There was a kind of relief in that, even though Nerra couldn't see why she should feel such a thing at the thought of human things being allowed to live. They didn't matter, not compared to the beauty and wonder of the dragons, the Perfected, even the Lesser.

For now, the destruction of the search continued. Dragons wheeled around the city, or perched her and there on its spires. They flew out into the countryside, and came back with cows or sheep between their jaws. Others simply plunged into the masses of the dead, snatching up soldiers off the Southern Kingdom who had opposed them. Again, Nerra had the sense of a small, foolish part of her being strangely disgusted by it, but the rest of her understood that it was simply the way the world worked. Human things who fought against dragon-kind were no use as anything *other* than food, after all.

Below her perch, the rest of the Perfected continued to guide the Lesser about their search. Nerra jumped down to join them, heading for the now broken library, trying to help in the search. She plunged down into the depths of the library, her enhanced vision letting her see even by the faint glow of light that made it in from above. The Lesser teemed around her, and for a moment, it seemed like far too many, their howls and growling turning it all into chaos that seemed to hem Nerra in, making her think about what it would be like to be torn apart by these beasts.

Then she pushed her mind out toward them, commanding them in their search, reminding herself that she was Perfected, the chosen of the dragon queen herself. She made her way through the library, looking out for the amulet, determined to find the one thing that might threaten them.

As she walked through it, Nerra could make out the destruction. Most of the bookcases had been torn down, so that they lay like fallen dominoes. Many of the books were burnt beyond recognition, with only charred covers left of some of them. Nerra kept going through the library, picking through the books, trying to find any sign of a space where the amulet might be hidden. She saw four cage-like structures around the perimeter of the library's interior, two of which seemed to be open already, bodies lying in front of them, torn open by what were obviously traps within.

Even as Nerra watched, the Lesser surged toward the others, tearing them open. She saw them fall, brought down by poison darts and slashing blades. Nerra stepped into those spaces in their wake, but still, there was no sign of the amulet that they sought.

Nerra. Shadr's mental voice was fainter at this greater distance, but it was still clear. This was not a connection that could be so easily broken. *Come back to me.*

Nerra could feel the urgency there, so she turned and pushed her way back through the ranks of the Lesser, heading back in the direction of the surface. The Lesser parted to let her through, clearing a path so that she could hurry upward, out into the open air.

Shadr was waiting there, in the middle of the open space in front of the library. She was alone, none of the Lesser or Perfected coming close to her, leaving a wide space of open ground around her. Even the other dragons were at a distance, circling in the air or perched atop buildings.

There was one approaching though, flying toward them straight as an arrow. Nerra saw the blue of its scales shining in the sun, saw it close in and land in a sweep of open wings. As it did so, Nerra realized that she knew this dragon. It was *hers*, the one whose egg she had found, out in the forest.

This one is not yours, Shadr said, and Nerra could feel the note of anger there under the surface. *You are mine, not Alith's.*

Nerra could feel the jealousy there, and the sudden tension. She put a hand on Shadr's flank.

"That isn't what I meant," she said softly, as the other dragon approached. Even so, Shadr reared up to her full height, looking down on Alith with such fury that the other dragon crouched low in submission. Nerra felt bad about that, not wanting to see the creature she had helped to bring into the world treated like that.

She caught the flicker of communication between Shadr and the blue-scaled dragon. Touching Shadr, she could make out some of it, the words and feelings flying fast.

I have found it, might queen, Alith sent.

Found what?

I have found the amulet, Alith sent, *the one that we seek.*

Nerra could feel Shadr's surprise. *Where? Show us.*

Images flickered through the link between her and Shadr. She recognized the sight of Royalsport below, seen through the eyes of a flying dragon. She saw the castle and the Houses, the separate islands and the city walls. Nerra felt the pull of the amulet through Alith's memories, there, and then gone, and then there again. She felt the pain that had come in the midst of a battle with the humans who had thrown magic up, dangerous as a dragon's breath, even if their bodies were soft and easy to devour.

She saw a man with hair the color of dragon flame. He was holding something aloft, and to Nerra's eyes he looked frightened, but maybe it was just that she could feel the fear coming through the link from Shadr and the other dragon. She saw the amulet in the human thing's hand, eight-sided and shining with the colors of dragon-kind. Nerra *felt* the push of the amulet's power for herself, the control that had sent Alith into battle against the human things in masks. She felt the way that Shadr pulled away in that moment, tearing free of the connection as if it hurt.

Nerra found that she was breathing hard in that moment, her body shaking with the memory of the control that had come from the amulet. At the time, it had felt like nothing, but now it felt as if some sticky substance were all over the scales of her skin, coating her and making her feel somehow unclean.

"That is … vile," Nerra said. "To control a dragon like that … I thought I understood before, but it's so much worse than I thought."

It is why I wanted to get to the amulet before humans could use it, Shadr sent.

Nerra bowed her head. "I'm sorry. I failed you, I guessed wrong about where it would be."

The reasons were sound enough, Shadr sent. *And you are mine. Any failure of yours is mine as well. I should have risked more, rather than coming here first.*

A ripple seemed to emanate from Shadr. Around her, the Lesser ceased their destruction; there was no point to it now that they knew that the amulet was not in Astare after all. They formed up behind those of the Perfected whose task it was to shepherd them, moving from the inner city out into the space beyond.

Even as they retreated from the inner city, the dragons came in, perching on buildings, looking down at Shadr and Nerra. Nerra could feel the dragon queen's displeasure, and something else as well: a hint of nervousness.

They are not happy that we did not find the amulet in time, Shadr sent. *They say that we should have gone the other way. They say that we should go that way now and that my Perfected should pay the price of failure.*

One of the dragons, with scales the deep gold of amber, dropped from one of the roofs toward Shadr. As if she had been expecting it, the great black dragon took to the air, slamming into the other dragon, claws drawing blood as they raked along its scales. The two dragons tangled in midair, tumbling and turning like two fighting cats, even while fire and shadow burst around them. Their roars were deafening, the impact of their bodies against one another resounding across the city.

The fight was brief, and it was brutal. In just seconds, the amber dragon was tumbling from the air, one wing ragged from Shadr's claws, a patch of its scales darkened by shadow fire. It fell to the ground and lay there, making pained sounds as Shadr stood over it in triumph.

I rule! The words echoed in Nerra's head, loud enough that it almost hurt. Around her, she saw several of the other dragons recoil, as Shadr made her way back to her.

"What was that?" Nerra asked.

A challenge, Shadr replied. *They wanted to do the next part their way, racing for the human city. They called me weak when I refused. I am not weak.*

"You are strong beyond all others," Nerra assured her, placing a hand on the dragon's flank. There was a spot there where a wound lay, and it pained Nerra even to see it. "Does this mean that we aren't heading to Royalsport?"

Not their way, Shadr replied. *If one has found the amulet, we must be more cautious. We must find that one, draw them out. We must kill them before they kill us. Only then can the rest proceed.*

Nerra understood then. In the space of one vision, this had gone from an easy conquest to something else, something far more dangerous. This was no longer about just taking back what had been lost. This was about survival now.

EPILOGUE

As dawn broke over the city, Anders sat atop the edge of a broken section of roof, admiring the blade that currently rested in his hands. As much as he hated to admit that Devin could do anything better than him, *this* was something he could never have made by himself. He was almost grateful to the other boy for that, even if Devin had proved himself too much of a coward to use the blade as intended to kill the dragon they had faced.

Anders would not hesitate when the time came. For now, though, he looked out over the city in the direction of the castle, and more specifically at the tower attached to its side. There was never any guarantee that the magus would be somewhere, but if he was going to be anywhere now, with all that was happening, it was there. It would take a lot of effort to get inside the castle unseen, but Anders was willing to risk it, for this.

He would go there, and he would wait for the sorcerer. He would give Master Grey a *reason* to appear. Then, when he did, Anders would kill him. He would kill him, finish things with Devin, and then fulfill the destiny that had been his all his life.

Slowly, Anders climbed down from the roof, heading for the castle. He made his way along streets strewn with rubble, fire-blackened timbers showing the aftermath of the dragon's attack. He found himself hoping that the family he'd helped would be able to find another place to live, especially as it was partly Anders's fault that the dragon had come their way at all. Perhaps when he was done, he would find them and give them coin for shelter.

For now, he kept walking, ignoring the people working to dig others out of the wreckage. He kept on through the city, up into its noble quarter, until he was only a short way from the castle. He paused, considering the guards on its gates, and the thickness of its walls.

He was still considering it when he felt something pull on the edges of his mind.

Anders felt the magic in that pull, felt the power there, and for a second he thought that it might be Master Grey. This was something different though, although something that still held a lot of power. Looking around in curiosity, he followed the feeling, tracking the magic the way a hound might track a scent.

It led him to the ruins of a wall, and Anders started to dig. He threw aside stones, large and small, pulling them out of his way, following the traces of the magic. He clasped his arms around a particularly large lump of rock, heaving it aside with a cry of effort.

Below, an amulet sat, eight-sided and shining.

Now Available for Pre-Order!

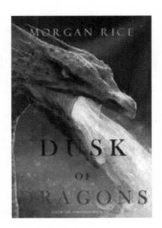

DUSK OF DRAGONS
(Age of the Sorcerers—Book Six)

"Has all the ingredients for an instant success: plots, counterplots, mystery, valiant knights, and blossoming relationships replete with broken hearts, deception and betrayal. It will keep you entertained for hours, and will satisfy all ages. Recommended for the permanent library of all fantasy readers."

—Books and Movie Reviews, Roberto Mattos (re The Sorcerer's Ring)

"The beginnings of something remarkable are there."

—San Francisco Book Review (re A Quest of Heroes)

From #1 bestseller Morgan Rice, author of A Quest of Heroes (over 1,300 five star reviews) comes a startlingly new fantasy series. DUSK OF

DRAGONS is book #6 in bestselling author Morgan Rice's new epic fantasy series, Age of the Sorcerers, which begins with book #1 (THRONE OF DRAGONS), a #1 bestseller with dozens of five-star reviews—and a free download!

In DUSK OF DRAGONS (Age of the Sorcerers—Book Six), the many storylines and characters finally converge, in a complex and epic battle for the very future of the capital and the kingdom.

Lenore leads her army for the capital, determined to avenge her mother and take it back from King Ravin. Devin, Renard, Erin and Greave each lead their own personal battles. Inside the gates, Aurelle and others aid the cause. And Grey oversees it all.

What follows is shocking and unexpected, with a series of twists that turn heroes into villains and villains into heroes in the fog of war.

But after a shocking twist that no one could have expected, even all of their efforts may not be enough.

Will the kingdom survive?

AGE OF THE SORCERERS weaves an epic sage of love, of passion, of sibling rivalry; of rogues and hidden treasure; of monks and warriors; of honor and glory, and of betrayal, fate and destiny. It is a tale you will not put down until the early hours, one that will transport you to another world and have you fall in in love with characters you will never forget. It appeals to all ages and genders.

Book #7 will be available soon.

"A spirited fantasy….Only the beginning of what promises to be an epic young adult series."

—Midwest Book Review (re A Quest of Heroes)

"Action-packed…. Rice's writing is solid and the premise intriguing."

DUSK OF DRAGONS
(Age of the Sorcerers—Book Six)

Did you know that I've written multiple series? If you haven't read all my series, click the image below to download a series starter!

Made in the USA
Middletown, DE
12 January 2022

58494001R00116